"There aren't many things I know how to do except please a man."

Gabe looked at Meg. "I think this is where we ought to part company. There's no telling what kind of trouble I'll run into."

"I'm going with you," Meg said.

"Wait for me here."

"Can't," she said. "We're almost broke. I'd have to go to work, and there aren't many things I know how to do except please a man."

"Hold up there!" a voice said. Gabe stiffened and turned to see a sheriff standing on the boardwalk.

"I got word that a man and woman escaped from the jail in El Paso. Would you be that pair?"

"Nope," Gabe replied.

The sheriff's hand reached for his gun, but Gabe's own left hand was already streaking across his waist, and he drew his Colt . . .

Also in the LONG RIDER Series

LONG RIDER
FAST DEATH
GOLD TOWN
APACHE DAWN
KILL CRAZY HORSE!
SHADOW WAR
THE GHOST DANCERS
HELLHOLE
THE LAND BANDITS
THE BUFFALO HUNTERS
KILLER MUSTANG
THE SANTA FE RING
VENGEANCE TOWN
THE COMANCHEROS
BLOOD HUNT
SNAKETOWN
TOWN TAMER

LONG RIDER

TEXAS MANHUNT

CLAY DAWSON

18

DIAMOND BOOKS, NEW YORK

TEXAS MANHUNT

A Diamond Book / published by arrangement with the author

PRINTING HISTORY
Diamond edition / March 1992

For information address: The Berkley Publishing Group, 200 Madison Avenue, New York, New York 10016.

ISBN: 1-55773-679-0

Diamond Books are published by The Berkley Publishing Group, 200 Madison Avenue, New York, New York 10016.

PRINTED IN THE UNITED STATES OF AMERICA

10 9 8 7 6 5 4 3 2 1

CHAPTER ONE

Gabe Conrad reined his weary sorrel gelding to a halt and stood up tall in his stirrups. His gray eyes, shaded by his sweat-stained and battered Stetson, surveyed the rugged chaparral and brush country of southwest Texas. The day before he'd crossed the Pecos River which, in late summer, hadn't been much more than a stream. Still, Gabe had filled his canteens and watered his horse, then drank all the water his own belly could hold. In this blistering part of the country, a man could die of thirst. He could also die of hunger or at the hands of Indians—if the Mexican banditos that frequently raided across the Rio Grande did not get to him first.

Gabe did not like the country that stretched out before him. It was a tortured, sun-blasted land best fit for rattlesnakes, scorpions, and tarantulas. True, there were some large cattle ranches, but they weren't prospering, and the Mexican banditos were rustling their cattle about as fast as they could be roped and branded.

As if sharing his low opinion of the country, his gelding snorted wearily and then closed its eyes. The animal, like himself, was accustomed to the Great Plains country where acres and acres of tall buffalo grass stretched on like a soft, swaying sea of green.

"It ain't pretty," Gabe said, "but from what I hear, El Paso might be even worse. Still, it's new country, and that makes it worth seeing and knowing."

The horse didn't seem impressed. Its hooves had to be sore, and it had dropped two hundred pounds since Gabe had ridden west out of Houston. He'd been offered a job in El Paso—not much of a job, but one that gave him some excuse to travel across new country. Big Jed Williams had asked Gabe to come live and work on his ranch outside El Paso where he'd be in charge of catching and breaking wild mustangs.

Gabe liked horses and was good with them. He could cowboy, shoe horses and mules, drive a stagecoach, and even mend fences if he had to, but it was horses that were his love. Williams had said that West Texas had a lot of good mustangs that needed roping and breaking. The rancher had promised Gabe he'd make twenty-five dollars for every one that he broke. That was good money for a bronc buster and, although money had never been the most important thing in Gabe's life, it was sometimes a good thing to have in an emergency.

"Let's get along," Gabe said, settling back down in his saddle and touching his spurs to the sorrel's flanks.

All the rest of the afternoon, Gabe pushed on over one low, hot hill after another. When sundown came and he still had not found a spring or a creek to water in and offer some grass for the sorrel, he made camp anyway. He watered the sorrel by filling his Stetson from his canteen. He hobbled the animal and told it to forage for itself as best it could.

"There's bound to be grain at the Williams Ranch," he said in apology, "and I'll see you get some fat back on your ribs."

Gabe took his Winchester and went hunting just at sundown. His feet were encased in moccasins, and he moved silently through the brush. When a cottontail sprang out from behind a rock and bounded off toward the Rio Grande, the Winchester slammed to Gabe's shoulder, and he shot the rabbit in midair.

Thirty minutes later, he was roasting the cottontail over his low campfire and gazing up at a starry sky. When he finally got sleepy, he reached into his saddlebags and pulled out his mother's old Bible. He read a few passages and then turned to a page where his mother, in her very tiny hand, had written a note in the margins. The note itself was not important, just something about how she admired a sunset and how her young son had played with the other Sioux children. The note was one of many in the Bible which was, along with Gabe's buffalo coat, all that he had to remind himself of his parents. He'd never known his father, but his mother, captured by the Sioux and treated like one of the tribe, had been his friend and his teacher.

Damn, Gabe thought, if she could see me down in this country now, she'd be wondering why I was such a fool to be so far from home. The memory of his mother and her scribbled words in the Bible comforted Gabe and reminded him once again that, although he was by blood a white man, he had been raised by the Sioux from birth and was, in spirit at least, Oglala Sioux.

Gabe returned the Bible to his saddlebags and was about to stretch out and go to sleep when his horse suddenly bolted and snorted with alarm. Instantly, Gabe was grabbing his Winchester and Colt .44 as he rolled sideways into the brush expecting either Indians or Mexican banditos to be creeping up, ready to kill him for what he owned.

"Hello the camp!" an anxious voice called from the inky darkness. "We come as friends."

Gabe did not trust strangers. He made no reply but lay still in the brush. Having been raised by the Oglala, he had learned the value of patience and knew that the most patient man often was the one that lived to see tomorrow's sunrise.

"Hello there!" someone shouted from the darkness. "I said we come as friends. We got a lame horse and a sick, feverish young woman. We're out of water and food. We could use some help, mister!"

The voice did sound desperate, but Gabe was not convinced. Shoving his rifle out before him, he wiggled through the brush until he could see the silhouettes of three horses and riders. Two of the riders were wearing Stetsons and the third a huge sombrero. One of their horses was pulling a travois, and Gabe thought he could see the outline of the sick woman.

"Raise your hands," Gabe shouted, punctuating his order with the sound of his Winchester's lever action.

"Aw fer cripessakes!" one of the riders complained. "We could have snuck up and killed you, but we helloed your camp. What the hell is the matter with you? Ain't you ever heard of Texas hospitality?"

Gabe stood up and slowly moved forward. His approach was so silent that it was not detected by the three men until he was just a few yards behind them.

"Keep your hands to the stars," he warned.

The men had the presence of mind to do as he ordered, and it was well that they did, for Gabe wasn't someone who made idle talk.

"What do you want?" he asked, stepping around to face them, rifle levelled.

The leader, a tall, cadaverous man whose hatchet-face was hidden in the shadow of his hat, said, "We already told you, mister. A little food, some water, and a helping hand would be appreciated."

"I have no food," Gabe told them. "I shot a cottontail at sundown, and I already ate it. As for water, I need what I have. The Pecos River is a day's ride away. You could be there by noon tomorrow."

"If we go riding off in that direction, the woman is going to die," the man said. "We're trying to reach Del Rio. There's a doctor there who ain't much, but he's this woman's only chance."

"That's right," the second man said, "but without water and a little rest . . . well, the woman ain't got a chance."

Gabe frowned. "What's wrong with her?"

"She was travelin' with us when a rattlesnake bit her horse. It threw her into some rocks and ran off. She's gone crazy in the head. Maybe something got busted inside."

"Can we put our hands down now, señor? The sky, she is getting very heavy to hold up."

Gabe turned to the Mexican. He was big and ugly and wore crossed bandoliers across his broad chest. Gabe counted three holsters and pistols, and he'd have bet anything that the man was also carrying at least a couple of knives and probably a hide-out pistol or two.

"All right," Gabe said, lowering his Winchester, "you can drop your arms and dismount. I've got two full canteens of water, and I can shoot a couple more rabbits tomorrow after sunrise. There's a little flour and corn in my saddlebags, some jerked beef that ain't worth much, and a couple pounds of sugar and coffee. You're welcome to as much as you need."

"Well, that's real kind of you," the tall, cadaverous man said as he dismounted and came over to stand before Gabe with his outstretched hand. "My name is Cass, this here is my friend, Ace, and the Mex is called Juara. What's your handle?"

"Gabe." He ignored the man's outstretched hand. Gabe had seen men tricked into having their gun hand tied up in a handshake while being shot, clubbed, or knifed.

Cass withdrew his hand. "You ain't a man that puts much trust in strangers, are you? Don't matter. Shows you're smart. Lots of men in this hard country would try to deceive you, then kill you for less than a Mexican peso."

"I've learned not to trust folks until I know 'em real well," Gabe said, not liking the appearance of any of the three.

Cass and Juara were dirty, unkempt men who would not meet his eyes directly, while Ace appeared to be the youngest, a handsome young dandy with bold, challenging eyes and an ivory-handled six-gun tied to his lean, muscular thigh. Ace, Gabe decided, was a gunfighter. All three looked plenty capable of murder.

"Then you're a smart man," Cass said. "Ace, why don't you make us some coffee? Sure could use some after so long."

"Why don't you make it yourself?" Ace drawled. "Or tell the Mex to do it." Even in the poor light of the stars, Gabe saw Cass stiffen with anger and the Mexican's black eyes narrow.

"Hell," Cass growled, shoving past Gabe, "I'll make it and I'll drink it, too."

"Who's the girl?" Gabe asked the two men who remained.

Juara didn't answer the question, but Ace liked the sound of his own voice too much to remain quiet. "She's my woman," he said. "We got hitched this spring over in New Orleans. Was gonna make a new start in California and was coming across Texas when that damned rattlesnake ruined everything."

For some reason, the story did not ring true. Maybe it was because Ace showed no real concern for the woman on the travois. Not once had he gone to her side since he'd dismounted. If the woman was his wife, he was sure as hell acting indifferent about her possible brain damage.

"Where did you all meet?" Gabe asked, turning slightly so that his back would not be turned toward Cass and he could see the man out of the corner of his eye.

"In Houston," Cass called to them. "We met in Houston. You know how there's safety in numbers. We were all going to El Paso. Ace and his wife were going on to California, but we were looking for work in El Paso. Isn't that right, boys?"

Ace and Juara nodded.

Cass found the coffee and then Gabe's pot. He also found a canteen and wasted no time in adding water and coffee, then setting the pot on the fire.

"Where you heading, Gabe?"

"I was also going to El Paso."

Cass forced a smile. "Why, that's good! We can all travel together for protection! There's Kiowa and even Apache raiding down in this part of the country. And if we ran into a band of banditos, we'd have a better chance of holding our own with four of us ready to fight."

Gabe frowned. "You said you were going to Del Rio. Where's that?"

"About thirty, forty miles south along the Rio Grande. Ain't much, but that doctor, he might be able to do something for Ace's poor wife. Damn shame and bad luck that her fool horse threw her right onto some rocks."

Gabe got one of his canteens and walked over to crouch beside the unconscious woman. He had not been able to study her clearly until now, and he was shocked to note that her face was battered black and blue and quite swollen.

"She doesn't look any too good," Gabe said quietly as his fingers touched her brow and noted that she was running a high fever. "Did she land face-first in the rocks, or what?"

There was a moment of hesitation to his question before Cass blurted, "By golly, that's exactly what she did. Yes sir! Lit right on her face. Her right boot got caught in the stirrup for a few moments and the horse dragged her, too. She's real beat up."

Gabe shook his head. The woman was wearing an old dress that had been mended too many times. The dress was badly torn and soiled. Her hair was tangled and filled with stickers, and her hands, face, arms, and legs were caked with dirt. She smelled, and it made him angry that she looked so unkempt, and that her husband had not taken better care of her since the accident.

Gabe stood up. "Let's get the travois untied and lower her to the ground. Ace, I expect you'll want to use some of this water to clean her up a little and cool her brow. She feels like she's on fire to me."

"Yeah," Ace said, coming over and taking the canteen from Gabe, then giving himself a long drink. "She feels hot to me, too. Think she'll live?"

"I don't know," Gabe said, starting to untie the travois, "but a bad head injury is often fatal. Best thing you can do for her is just try and keep her fever down."

"Hard to do without water," Ace said, "and water is in real short supply."

Anger flared in Gabe. "She's your wife, and it's my water I'm offering for free. So I guess if you don't want it all to drink for yourself, we can spare most of this canteen."

Ace stiffened. His hand moved closer to his gun, and he hissed, "Mister, this may be your camp and your canteen I'm holding, but you'd better watch your manners if you know what's good for you. I noticed that your trigger finger of your right hand is twisted all cockeyed—but mine damn sure ain't."

Gabe tore the canteen from the gunfighter's grip, and his own hand dropped down near his six-gun. It was true that his trigger finger was broken and twisted, but he could still use his left hand to make a cross draw that had beaten more than one so-called "gunfighter" who would still be watching his stationary right hand, while his left was already in action.

"Ace, let it be!" Cass said. "This ain't the time to be fightin'!"

Gabe was furious, but he didn't let his anger show as he stared at the handsome young gunfighter.

"I guess we'd better do what we can for your wife," he said in a flat, hard voice.

Ace relaxed and then turned away saying, "You just leave her be, mister. Keep your damn hands off of her."

Gabe shook his head with disbelief. What kind of man would treat his wife that way? No kind of man at all, was the answer. Gabe knelt beside the woman and gently pried open her mouth so that he could pour water down her parched gullet. He kept one eye on the woman and one eye on Ace, to see if he would interfere.

But a man only has two eyes, and that was Gabe's undoing. The big Mexican was standing close, and the moment Gabe took his eyes off of Ace, Juara punched him in the side of the head so hard that Gabe was knocked sprawling. Before he could recover, Juara landed on him like a boulder and hit him again. Gabe tried to twist out from under the weight of the Mexican. As he struggled, he heard the sound of running boots and turned to see Ace standing over him.

"So long, Mr. Do-gooder," Ace said with a wicked grin. "It's going to feel real good to kick your head in."

Gabe bucked like a crazy man as Ace very deliberately drew back his foot and kicked the side of Gabe's head like he would a dog.

Red and yellow lights exploded behind Gabe's eyes along with a terrible pain as he dimly heard Cass laugh and shout,

"Kick his goddamn head off, Ace! Kick it clean off his neck!"

Gabe didn't hear any more as, mercifully, he lost consciousness.

CHAPTER TWO

When Gabe awoke in a sea of agony, he could not focus his eyes. The rocks and brush around him seemed to swirl and waver. When he grunted and rolled over onto his back, the sun spun lazily in the sky and pinpoints of orange light kept exploding in his brain. Gabe's hand fluttered up to block out the sun, and it took all of his strength to lift his arm. His mouth was caked with blood, and when he squinted his face felt as if it were sun-cracked mud. His forearm dropped across his eyes, and he moaned and lay still, wanting nothing more than to drift back into a merciful sleep. But the sun grew hotter, and Gabe's throat ached for water. His body was bathed in sweat, and ants crawled on his flesh and stung him.

Gabe rolled back onto his belly and took several deep breaths. He squeezed his eyes shut and tried to form a single coherent thought, and when he failed at that, his instincts told him that he must get up and search for water and shelter from the burning sun.

Pushing himself to his hands and knees, he grit his teeth and grunted with pain. Taking deep breaths, he lunged to his feet and swayed like a tree about to topple under the ax. But he did not fall. Instead, he took one half-blind step after another, and the act of walking somehow did clear his mind.

There were four sets of hoofprints leading southwest toward the Rio Grande and Old Mexico. Gabe twisted around to look back at his camp. His old saddlebags had been rifled and pitched into the brush. Slowly he retrieved them and sighed with relief to discover that his mother's Bible had not been taken.

"Why would men like that take a Bible anyway?" he whispered brokenly.

Everything else of value had been taken from him—his rifle, his six-gun, food, canteens, horse, saddle, and blankets. Everything except the saddlebags, the old Sioux buffalo robe vest that he had made from his mother's last tipi, and a few clothes and cooking utensils. Gabe walked like a man who'd drank too much tequila as he slowly gathered up his belongings, found his Stetson, and eased it down over his battered skull. Now that he was fully awake, he could feel how swollen the right side of his face was. His right eye was puffed almost shut.

Cass or Ace had also kicked him a few times in the ribs, and they hurt like hell, but Gabe did not think they were broken. Gathering his supplies, he turned south and followed the hoofprints. He concentrated on them and them alone. The sun grew hotter, but he kept moving one foot after another until time itself lost all meaning.

By sundown, he was weaving from side to side, half-delirious with the need for water. His tongue felt swollen and his lips had cracked and bled. Gabe knew that he had to keep walking. If he stopped and allowed himself to sleep, he didn't think he would awaken in the morning.

"Move," he croaked in a voice that he did not recognize. "Don't stop moving."

All that night, Gabe moved steadily south, his back to the North Star, his eyes straight ahead as he followed the tracks in the moonlight. The three men who had left him for dead had not even considered that he might survive their inhuman beating and follow them on foot. They had abandoned the travois and probably tied the sick woman on Gabe's sorrel. He wondered if the woman was dead by now. He also wondered if she had been beaten like himself instead of thrown from horseback as they had claimed. It did not matter. Gabe knew that if somehow he survived, he would track the three men down if it took the rest of his life. He would find and kill them one by one, and he would save the young woman if at all possible.

"I don't believe that she was his wife," he said, over and over to himself. "I think they kidnapped her, probably used her, and then beat her half to death. I think that is the real truth."

This thought, that he might be struggling to save not only himself but also the woman, gave Gabe extra determination. He would walk until he fell, and when he could not stand any more, then he would crawl and then slither until the last spark of life left his body. By dawn he *was* crawling and hallucinating. The hoofprints he followed seemed to be alive, things moving along ahead of him, always just out of his reach.

Gabe followed the hoofprints right down the north bank of the Rio Grande until they disappeared into the water. It took him several seconds to realize that he was wet, and when he did, Gabe collapsed in the warm, muddy water and drank until his stomach was full. He floated in the water for almost an hour, luxuriating in its refreshing, life-restoring power. When at last he stood up and sought the shade of some nearby cottonwood trees, his mind was clear again, and he knew that, somehow, he would survive.

Gabe was beyond hunger by that next evening. He had stoned several lizards and eaten them raw, but they hadn't been that filling. He was still trailing the hoofprints that had turned west to follow the river, and was very intent on them until he almost stepped on a thick, four-foot long rattlesnake. The snake's ominous rattle warned Gabe just in time, and he quickly found a rock. Being unsteady, he had to find several more rocks until he finally managed to bash the reptile's head into the sand.

Gabe chewed away the snake's head, then ripped its skin off with his teeth and ate the meat. He gulped it down while the snake was still warm and wriggling, and when he finished, he was satisfied and knew that he would be strong for a second night of walking.

Many times that second night, Gabe would throw his aching body into the river and revive himself enough to push on for a few more hours. His only hope was to overtake the men who had robbed and beaten him, then left him for dead. But by midnight, it became clear that the men were, themselves, pushing on through this night.

An hour after dawn, he saw the horse. At first, Gabe thought that his eyes must be playing some cruel joke on him. But the horse was no joke, and it was very tame. In fact, when it saw Gabe, it came plodding in his direction, nickering softly.

"Easy boy," Gabe said, placing his hand on the animal's muzzle, then scratching behind its ears. It wasn't much of a horse. It was a thin bay gelding with a slight swayback. Its muzzle was flecked with gray hair. Spots of white hair behind its high withers were the remnant marks of old saddle sores, and the gelding's feet were chipped and in bad shape.

"Looks like you could use my help almost as much as I could use yours," Gabe told the horse.

The gelding nodded as if it understood and rubbed Gabe's chest with its bony head. Gabe used strips of his own shirt to fashion a very crude bridle. If the horse had not been extremely gentle and patient, it would never have allowed itself to be controlled or even mounted. But once Gabe was astride the beast, he drummed his heels against its ribs and forced the gelding into a hammering trot that almost caused him to black out with the pain in his head.

"Slow down," Gabe told himself. "You got plenty of time to catch them. They aren't expecting any company, and even if you did overtake them, you're in no shape to do anything but get yourself killed."

What he said made good sense, but it was hard being patient. Now that he was mounted, even on an old scrub horse that nobody would have wanted, every instinct in his pain-racked body wanted him to hurry, to catch the three men and to save the woman from their clutches. But Gabe's iron will prevailed, and he slowed the old, stumbling gelding with the bad hooves. He'd find them all right. It was just a matter of when and where.

To Gabe's surprise, the tracks he followed veered northwest late that afternoon, away from the river. He could not figure that out. In this country, water was life. Gabe sighed and pondered a very important decision. If he left the river and the men he followed were stupid, then he and they might perish of thirst out in the high chaparral. But what choice did he have but to follow the tracks? And besides, the men must have had a reason to leave the river.

Gabe reined the old horse away from the Rio Grande and followed the tracks. At dusk, he saw a horseman up ahead. The man was coming from the southwest at a high lope, and Gabe knew he was not one of the men that he was following.

"Hello there!" Gabe shouted, his voice brittle.

The man saw him now and changed directions. He came toward Gabe still at a lope, and as he drew close, he yanked out his six-gun and bellowed, "Hands up, you sorry son of a bitch, or I'll finish off what's left of you!"

"Now wait—"

Gabe's protest died on his lips as the man sent a bullet burning the air beside his ear. Gabe's hands went up, and the old bay horse stumbled to a grateful halt.

"You're under arrest!" the man said.

"For what?"

"For stealing Judge Roy Bean's old bay horse, damn you. I been huntin' that sorry son of a bitch for three days, and I got to tell you, I ain't any happier about this than the judge will be."

"But I didn't steal him!"

"Oh yeah, well, you sure as hell didn't buy him! You got a receipt or a bill of sale from the judge? Hell no, you don't!"

"This horse was half-dead when I found him wandering beside the Rio Grande."

"Get down and put your hands behind your back, mister. I'm arresting you in the name of the law. I'm one of the judge's deputies, and I'm taking you to Langtry for sentencing, and most likely hanging."

"This is insane!" Gabe cried, dropping to the ground. "I was robbed of my own horse, beaten almost to death, and left for dead. When I walked and crawled after the three men that wronged me, I found this horse. I was going after them. Look at their tracks!"

"I saw them tracks. But you're the man with the stolen horse."

"But—"

"Shut up or I'll put you to sleep with the butt of my six-gun! The judge sent me out to find his horse, and I found him with you ridin' him. That's all I know. It'll be up to the judge what happens to you, mister. So tell your story to Roy Bean."

"But the men I follow have a very sick woman. They'll get away clean if you don't help me find them."

"Let 'em! I've been out in this damned country hunting that worthless horse of the judge's for three days, and I need a drink and a woman, in that order."

The deputy tied Gabe's hands behind his back. The man was tall, in his forties, with a potbelly and rotted teeth. He stunk, and yet Gabe supposed that he looked downright pretty in comparison to himself. The deputy led the old bay gelding over to a rock.

"I can't believe that you were using rags for a bridle," he groused as he removed his lariat from his saddle and quickly made a rope halter. "You are the sorriest-looking horse thief I've ever seen in my life."

"I told you that the horse came to me. He was in such bad shape I figured that someone must have turned him loose. Either that, or he wandered off and wasn't worth looking for."

The deputy shook his head. "Mister, if you insult the judge's horse to his face like that, he'll order you strung up by the neck with barbed wire instead of doing it nice with a hangman's noose so your neck snaps. I'm just giving you fair warning."

"Who the deuce is this Judge Roy Bean?" Gabe growled. "I never even heard of him."

The deputy moaned. "Mister, you'll have no chance at all with a remark like that. My advice to you is to fall to your knees and beg for mercy and forgiveness. Beg for a quick necktie party."

"But I'm innocent!" Gabe shouted. "Look at me. See my face? Do you think I did that to myself just for the hell of it? Someone beat and robbed me. I found this horse and was trying to catch up with them."

"To do what? Throw rocks at them?" The deputy actually chuckled. "Mister, you have no idea how bad you look right now. The judge will be doing you a favor to put a noose around your neck."

"I'd like to be the one who decides on that," Gabe said.

"Well, you won't be," the deputy vowed. "And Judge Roy Bean, he sure is going to be mad about you stealing his favorite old horse. Had that bay when he first arrived in this country. Sort of sentimental about Old Buck, if you know what I mean."

Gabe shook his head. He followed the deputy and "Old Buck" to a rock and hopped onto the gelding's bony back.

"How far to Langtry?" he asked.

"We'll be there by morning. But if I was going to swing, I'd be in no hurry." The deputy chuckled again as he climbed onto his own horse.

Gabe didn't say anything more because he'd only be wasting his breath. He just hoped that Judge Roy Bean wasn't as ruthless and unreasonable as this deputy made him out to be. If he was, the game was over.

CHAPTER THREE

Langtry, Texas, wasn't a city, or a even much of a town. It was just a run-down watering hole near the Rio Grande. There was a line of decrepit shacks, some corrals, a dilapidated general store, a livery, and a sign that told everyone that the Southern Pacific Railroad would one day be coming through Langtry on its way between San Antonio and El Paso.

But until the railroad actually arrived, there wasn't much to see in Langtry, and the only real building of any note was a single-storied structure with a big veranda, a bunch of indolent Mexicans and cowboys sitting in chairs, and a sign reading:

JUDGE ROY BEAN
JUSTICE OF THE PEACE
NOTARY PUBLIC
and the LAW WEST OF THE PECOS

When the deputy brought Gabe up the main street, the Mexicans and cowboys who dozed in the shade of the veranda hardly bothered to raise their heads out of curiosity. A mangy dog got up and scratched, then sauntered down the street. That was the extent of Gabe's greeting to Langtry.

The saloon had a few other signs tacked onto it in no particular order. Gabe read that beer cost a nickel, whiskey ten cents, and that the saloon was called the Jersey Lilly.

"Funny name for a saloon," Gabe commented.

The deputy reined his horse to a standstill before the Jersey Lilly and dismounted, stiffness reflected in his every movement.

"It's named in honor of Miss Lillie Langtry," the deputy said. "Just like the town. You've heard of Miss Langtry, haven't you?"

"Can't say as I have," Gabe confessed. "Who is she?"

The deputy groaned. "Man, you are an ignorant son of a bitch! Ain't nobody that ain't heard of the most beautiful, the most talented woman in the whole universe! She's a great actress on Broadway and the London stage. She's also a famous singer."

Gabe slid off his horse. "Well, I never heard of her," he said, "but then, I don't go to many theaters. In fact, I've never been to a single one."

The deputy sighed. "I guess the judge will probably tell you all about Miss Lillie before you hang. He might even show you one of the posters he has of her. I don't know. But if he does, you'd better be respectful."

"I'm always respectful of ladies," Gabe said. "But in truth, the only lady I'm thinking about right now is that poor woman that was in the company of the three men who robbed and beat me."

"She was probably just sick like those men told you," the deputy drawled. "Come on, let's go in and see if the judge is fit to hold court on you."

"Why wouldn't he be?"

The deputy did not answer the question. He nodded to several of the men on the porch and pushed Gabe through the front door into the Jersey Lilly.

Gabe took the big room in at a single glance. It was a saloon not unlike hundreds of others that he'd seen, with a bar, faro and poker tables, and battered brass spittoons. The bartender was a large man with a silver beard and penetrating brown eyes. He looked to be in his sixties and was wearing a white apron.

"Judge," the deputy said, "I got Old Buck tied up to the hitching post outside, but he looks to be in real poor shape, sir."

Judge Roy Bean finished polishing the glass in his big fist, all the while staring at Gabe. "What'd you arrest him for?"

"He was ridin' Old Buck north."

"Now wait a minute," Gabe interrupted. "I can explain. You see—"

"Save it for your trial," Bean growled, removing his apron and then reaching under the bar for a black, alpaca coat. He pulled it on while he moved around the bar and waddled heavily to the front door where he stood for several moments studying his old gelding.

"Boys," he said, "you all come inside. Court is in session."

Gabe had a bad feeling when everyone trooped inside and drinks were poured all around. That feeling did not improve when the judge asked his deputy, "How much money was he carrying?"

"Not one cent, Your Honor."

"No horse of his own or even a saddle?"

"Nope."

"Well dammit!" the judge groused. "What about a good rifle or pistol?"

"No sir. He was unarmed. Claims he'd been beaten, robbed, and left for dead. The only thing he had was his old saddlebags, a Bible, and a buffalo vest."

"And my fine bay gelding," the judge snapped with irritation.

"Yes sir, Old Buck and him were heading north."

Bean drew his six-gun and pounded its butt sharply against his bar top. "All right, everybody. Finish your drinks and put your glasses empty on the table. The Law West of the Pecos is now in session."

All eyes turned to Gabe who knew that he did not make a very impressive figure with his swollen and discolored face.

"Let's hear your story," the judge demanded.

"Well," Gabe began, "I was camped out in the brush when three men came out of the dark, dragging a travois on which lay a very feverish woman."

"Did you see her face? Was she good lookin' or an ugly woman?" the judge asked.

"She was young and pretty. Had yellow hair, but it was all dirty and matted with stickers. She'd been beaten up, and when I asked what happened, they told me she'd been thrown from her horse into rocks, then dragged a little. I had no reason then to doubt the story."

"But you do now."

"Yes, sir. Wouldn't you doubt it if those same men had beaten and robbed you, then left you to die without water?"

"I'll ask the questions," Bean snapped. "Deputy? What did you see?"

"I didn't see no travois, Judge. Didn't see no three men and a woman either."

Gabe protested. "But you saw their tracks."

"I saw some tracks. Lots of tracks. Figured they were made by vaqueros or cowboys searchin' the range for cimarrónes or maybe even mustangs."

"But Your Honor," Gabe protested, "I pleaded with your deputy to help me overtake the men who had robbed and beaten me. All I wanted was to use his gun, and I'd have brought them either to justice or Boot Hill. And I'd have saved the woman."

"I don't believe there even was a woman," Bean said. "All I know for sure was that you were riding my best horse north in the opposite direction of Langtry. Is that true, or is it not?"

"Yeah, it's true," Gabe said. "But—"

"The penalty for horse thievin' is to be hanged by the neck until dead," the judge said, cutting off Gabe's protest. "My deputy was under orders to find Old Buck and bring him back. He's done this and shall be rewarded."

The deputy grinned. "He's got a good pair of boots, Your Honor. Might be your size."

Bean stepped around his bar to study Gabe's boots. "Yeah," he said, "but they look a little small. What size do you wear, mister?"

"Go to hell!" Gabe exploded. "You're not getting my boots!"

"You're the one that's going to hell, and I will wear them boots if I can get my feet into them," Bean said with anger in his voice.

"But I'm innocent!"

"Not in the eyes of the law. I hereby sentence you to hang by the neck until dead. That is my ruling."

Gabe swallowed noisily. "This isn't a court of law," he said. "This isn't anything more than a mockery."

The judge slammed the butt of his six-gun down on the bar top. "I might have reconsidered your case, mister. But you just insulted the wrong man. Hanging will take place tomorrow morning at eight o'clock. This court is dismissed. Deputies, take this man out and chain him next to Bruno.

Bring his boots back here to me, and then we'll have a round on the house."

Almost everyone in the room seemed to be a deputy, or maybe it was simply that the judge expected them to help out in order to earn their free round of whiskey. All Gabe knew for certain was that he was overpowered by a swarm of "deputies", and any thoughts he might have had about making a run for it were immediately forgotten. He was shoved and half carried out the back door and unceremoniously dumped on the hard ground next to what might have been the only full-grown tree in town. Gabe was shackled by his ankle after his boots were torn roughly from his feet. A moment later, all the deputies rushed back into the Jersey Lilly like a bunch of starving cattle rushing for the feed bin. Only then did Gabe notice he was shackled beside a big black bear.

The bear also wore a leg iron and didn't seem a bit surprised to have company. It was lying on its stomach, head resting on its big paws. Its dark little eyes surveyed Gabe for a moment, then the bear gave a big yawn and went back to dozing away the rest of the afternoon.

"So you're Bruno," Gabe said.

The bear opened one eye, then closed it and went to sleep. Gabe wasn't too worried about the bear for he'd seen many in traveling frontier tent shows and acts. He didn't like the idea of chaining a bear up to a tree, but its fate seemed far more promising than his own, so he gave the matter little thought as he eased his spine up against the tree and studied the iron clamp and chain attached to his ankle.

The iron ankle-clamp was so tight it ached, and when Gabe had a better look at the locking mechanism, he knew that he wasn't going to break it open with anything less than a blacksmith's tools. The chain was just as heavy and wound around the tree which was at least twenty feet tall.

"I'm stuck," Gabe said. "I'd have more luck breaking out of a jail cell."

Gabe closed his eyes and considered the situation as calmly as he could from every angle. It seemed as if the only law in this town was that of Judge Roy Bean. That meant that he could not expect any real justice, for it seemed obvious that Bean was a man whose harsh sentencing was based entirely on emotion instead of the legal statutes.

Gabe sadly concluded that there was no chance of bringing any fresh evidence out in his behalf. The evidence of his story had ridden north and might be halfway to San Angelo by now, and it was also entirely possible that the feverish woman was dead.

"Things could not look worse," he said out loud as the bear began to snore and snort fitfully.

The remainder of the day passed very slowly for Gabe. He could hear Judge Roy Bean and his deputies drinking and raising hell in the Jersey Lilly. Every ten or fifteen minutes, one of them would stagger out the back door, study him, and then stumble forward a little ways only to take a leak.

One man, a mean-looking sort with a bad knife scar down the right side of his face, seemed drunker than the others. He boldly wove his way close to Gabe and sneered down at him.

"I think I'll piss on you," he announced, reaching for his fly.

Gabe tensed. If he could get the man's six-gun then perhaps a way might be found to shoot the chain apart and make an escape attempt.

"What do you think of that?" the man said, grinning broadly as he drew himself out of his pants.

Gabe knew that he had to get his man a little closer and from hard experience, he was sure that the best way to egg a bully on was to pretend cowardice.

"Please don't," he said, pushing himself up against the tree as if he were repulsed and beaten. "Give a fella a little dignity during his last hours."

The man laughed coarsely. "You sure ain't much, are you? Damn fool! If you'd stolen any other horse in all of southwest Texas the judge might have let you off if you'd had a little money. Bail money—that's what he really wants."

"I don't have any money."

"Don't you even know somebody that would lend you some?"

"No," Gabe said in a dejected voice.

"Well then, you're hardly worth pissing on, but I'm going to do it anyhow."

Gabe recoiled, and the man laughed. Emboldened now, he took two more steps forward, and that was all that Gabe needed to swing his foot out and strike the man behind his knee and bring him crashing to the ground.

"Hey, what the . . ."

The taunting deputy had his limp manhood in his left hand and was trying to draw his gun with his right hand when Gabe's fist exploded against the point of his jaw. The man's eyes rolled up into his forehead, and his entire body went limp.

Gabe wasted no time unholstering the man's six-gun. He checked to make sure that the gun was fully loaded, then he placed the barrel of the pistol against one of the links of chain and pulled the trigger. The chain jumped from Gabe's hand. It was dented but not broken.

"Damn!" Gabe swore, grabbing the chain again and taking aim.

The second bullet also failed to break the heavy chain and, by now, Bruno was on his feet and wailing like a dog.

Gabe heard the back door to the Jersey Lilly slam open as men piled out with their guns drawn. Gabe spun around to face them.

"Hold it!" Gabe shouted. "Drop your guns."

The deputies were pretty drunk by now but not so drunk that they were ready to open fire on their prisoner.

"Think about it," Gabe snapped. "I got nothing to lose because I've been sentenced to hang tomorrow anyway. I've got four bullets left in this pistol, and I'll take four men with me if need be."

There were at least fifteen of them, and they all started glancing sideways at each other.

"Who's got the damn key to this thing?" Gabe shouted. "I want the key!"

"I'm afraid that you can't have it," Judge Roy Bean said from the doorway. "No prisoner has ever escaped from my shackles, and you are not going to be the first to do so now."

The deputies parted to reveal the judge standing in the back doorway with a double-barreled shotgun pointed at Gabe.

"It's a standoff," Gabe said. "I'm not handing over this pistol, and you're not handing over the key. So where do we go from here?"

The judge shrugged his shoulders. "Me, I'm going back inside to have a drink. How about it, boys? One more round, and then we'll call it a night."

"Hey!" Gabe shouted.

The judge had been about to turn around, but now he stopped and raised his eyebrows in question. "Oh," he said. "You're wondering what will happen next. Well, after we have a drink, I'll have a couple of us get Winchesters, and go out there on the prairie and see who can put bullets in you first. 'Course, we'll be out of pistol range."

Gabe knew he was in trouble, but there was something that gave a man extra incentive when he knew that his next words would earn him either life or death.

"I'll hide behind your damn pet bear, Judge. You want to take long-distance target practice on me, you'll have to risk killing Bruno."

The judge's cheeks flamed with outrage. "You're a callous monster! You'd do that to a pet bear?"

"Damn right I would," Gabe said. "I've been convicted of a crime that I did not commit. The real horse thieves and outlaws are still riding north with a sick woman. They're the ones that you ought to be hanging tomorrow instead of me."

The judge looked at Bruno who made a soft woofing sound, as if begging for some give and take in this stalemate.

"All right, what were their names?"

Hope flickered in Gabe's heart. "The leader was a hatchet-faced man named Cass. He had a handsome young friend named Ace and a Mexican named—"

"Ace Randolph?" the judge asked quickly.

"He didn't give me his last name."

One of the deputies said, "Cass Hanson is said to be raiding up north. I heard Ace was with him these days."

"What was the Mexican's name?" the judge demanded.

"Juara," Gabe said.

"Juara Escobar?"

"I don't know," Gabe said.

"What'd he look like?"

"Big and ugly. Had a fist-busted nose. Wore a couple of bandoliers across his chest and at least three pistols on his hips. Rode a buckskin mare."

The judge and the deputies gaped. "That's Juara Escobar, all right," Bean said. "He's one of the most ruthless banditos in Mexico. As for the rest, well, I had a report from the Texas Rangers that three men—one a big Mexican and very likely Juara Escobar—had robbed a bank over in Houston. Nothin' was said about no woman, but the descriptions fit."

Gabe felt as if a mountain had lifted from his shoulders. "Then I guess you can see that I'm innocent and that everything I've told you is true."

"Not entirely," the judge said. "Two wrongs don't make no right. You still stole my old bay gelding. The fact that three desperados stole your own horse don't make your crime any less of an crime. You still committed a hangin' offense."

Gabe drew a deep breath. "Two wrongs don't make a right for certain," he argued, "but hangin' a man for trying to get back what was his don't sound like justice to me. And if someone don't go after those three, they'll get away clean."

Judge Roy Bean turned around to look at his men. "Any you deputies want to go after them three?"

The deputies clearly did not. They toed the dirt, took a sudden interest in their hands, and generally gazed around as if they'd never seen the back of the Jersey Lilly.

"Guess I got my damn answer!" The judge was angry. "Why if you ain't the sorriest excuse for a bunch of deputies I've ever seen! You'll belly up to my bar and talk a damn good story, every last yellow-bellied one of you. And you're all great for arresting each other when you're drunk and takin' in a cut of the bail money, but by God, when it comes to going after a real bunch of hard cases, you're all a bunch of cowards!"

The deputies shrank back from the judge who was known to go into dangerous rages.

"Give me one damn man who has the guts to go after them three. One man among you!"

No one would even meet the judge's eye.

"I'll go after them and I'll bring them back dead or alive," Gabe said.

The judge swung around and glared at him. "Sure, you'll say any damn thing to keep from hanging. And the minute you put Langtry behind, you'll raise the dust for parts unknown."

"No, I won't," Gabe said. "I'll give you my word of honor."

"Honor don't bring back prisoners," the judge groused. "No deal."

Gabe frowned. "All right," he said. "I'll tell you a little secret. My mother was captured by the Sioux, and I was raised by them. Mother was killed when the cavalry raided her camp, and the only thing I have to remember her by is her Bible and that buffalo robe vest. They mean more to me than anything in the world. You can hold onto them while I'm doing your work on the outlaw trail."

The judge glanced sharply at him. "There was a Bible. And you're wearing that vest did make me suspicious since it's so damned hot."

Still holding his gun on the unpredictable judge, Gabe reached into his back pocket and took out the Bible. It was badly frayed and the leather cover was half worn to pieces.

"Take a look at my mother's notes inside," he said, extending the Bible to the judge. "You'll be the only man I ever showed this too because it's so personal. But I guess seeing as how you hold my life in your hands, Mother wouldn't object."

"A Bible in one hand, a gun in the other," Bean snapped. "You sure are a man torn up the middle. Let me see it."

The judge took the Bible from Gabe and slowly leafed through it. His lips sometimes moved as he read one of the passages. Once, he said, "I can't read this line."

"What page?"

"One-nineteen."

"Oh yes," Gabe said, for it had taken him nearly a year to decipher that line. "It says, the Lord giveth and He taketh away pretty fast and when we're least expecting it."

"Hmmm," Bean mused, "yeah, I guess that is what it says."

"Have we got a deal?"

"Would you really have hidden behind old Bruno?"

"If forced to it," Gabe said, then added quickly, "but only as a last resort. I like bears myself."

"You do?"

"Yep. I like all animals."

"So do I," Bean growled, throwing a hard glance at his cowering men. "I like 'em a sight better than people."

The judge handed Gabe back his Bible. "All right," he said. "We'll go inside and have us a few drinks, and then we'll work out the terms."

"I don't drink hard liquor," Gabe said.

"What?"

"It's true."

"Well, if that ain't the damndest, sorriest thing I ever heard of. Why the hell not?"

"It makes men fools. Strong men go weak, and weak men get foolishly brave. I figure that it don't do men any good at all. Be a lot less murderin' and hell-raising if hard spirits were against the law of the land."

"Be a lot less fun, too," the judge said. "Besides whores, whiskey, good dogs and good horses, I don't know what else a man could rightly look forward to out in this country."

Gabe had to agree. It was a hard country, not fit for man nor beast, but he wisely decided not to tell the judge his opinion.

"All right," Bean said, tossing his shotgun to one of his deputies and producing the key to the shackles. "Come on inside. Maybe I can find some sarsaparilla or soda pop for you."

"A cup of water will do fine," Gabe said. "And my boots?"

"Give him his boots back," the judge ordered. "Didn't fit me anyway."

When the shackles were removed, Gabe shoved his gun in his holster, put on his boots, and followed the judge inside. The other men started to follow them into the Jersey Lilly, but Judge Bean roared and cussed at them so they slunk away.

"Sit down," the judge said, pouring himself a drink and dragging a bottle of soda from under the bar. "We got terms to decide. I set the terms, you agree to follow them. Is that understood?"

"You're holding all the cards in this game, not to mention my mother's Bible."

"That's right," the judge said. "And don't you ever forget it. Now, I want all three brought back alive."

"Not likely," Gabe said. "They're too tough. I might get lucky and capture them alive, but it's doubtful."

"If they're alive, I can collect a bounty for us. If you kill them, I want their heads brought back in a gunnysack. I don't guess you'd like doing that."

"I won't do it," Gabe said. "But I will try to capture rather than kill them."

The judge was not pleased. "You sure ain't the most cooperative man I ever dealt with."

"Neither are you."

"I'll loan you a horse," Bean said. "A good horse."

"Not Old Buck?"

"I said Old Buck was a good horse, but more like an old

friend. You'll need a young horse."

"A fast, sound, and strong horse," Gabe said. "And a Winchester rifle to replace the one that was taken from me. And a pistol."

"You already found another pistol," the judge said. "The rest will be waiting for you in the morning."

"Then we have a deal," Gabe said. "I'll strike out at daylight and pick up the trail where I was arrested. With any luck, I can overtake them in a week or two. I might even be back by the end of the month."

"Are you good and tough? Ruthless and fast on the gun? 'Cause if you ain't, then I'm backin' a dead man. And I don't back losers."

"I'm man enough to do the job," Gabe said simply. "I got my own reasons to get those three."

"Yeah," Bean said, "I can see that every time I look at your poor face."

Judge Roy Bean tossed down his whiskey and drawled, "Now tell me a thing or two about yourself."

Gabe frowned. "If you don't mind, I'd rather get some sleep. It'll be the last I'll get for a while."

Bean nodded. "All right. You can sleep in an empty room in the back. I'll see you in the morning."

"Bet on it," Gabe said. As he started to leave, the judge poured himself another drink and said, "I thought I had some good men for deputies. But them sorry bunch of bastards sure showed me otherwise."

"Don't be so hard on them," Gabe said. "Nobody wants to brace a man that has nothing to lose."

"Yeah," Bean said, "I guess you've got a good point there. See you in the morning."

Gabe left the man. Fifteen minutes later, he was sound asleep and dreaming of revenge against the three men who had almost gotten him hanged.

CHAPTER FOUR

Cass reined his horse to a standstill just outside of El Paso and waited while the others caught up to him. He did not like to wait on anyone for any reason but, under the circumstances, there was no sense in getting sore.

They'd had a long, brutal ride across hot, dangerous country. The horses were played out, and everyone's nerves were frayed.

They'd been jumped by Apache up near the Big Bend country and damned near lost their scalps. But, fortunately, they'd had enough guns and ammunition to hold off the attack and escape before more Apache arrived.

When Ace and Juara overtook him, Cass looked at the young woman. She'd come a long way toward recovery. If she hadn't been able to hang onto a running horse, the Apache would have had her for certain.

"How's the woman?"

"Can't you tell?" Ace said. "She's about ready to fall off her horse."

"We'll find a hotel room and hole up for a few days before we push on toward California," Cass said.

Juara ran his big hand across his horse's sweaty neck. "My mare is about finished. She's going to need a week before I go on."

"Too long," Cass said. "There are Texas Rangers hunting all over the state for us. The sooner we put a few hundred miles of Texas border behind us, the better off we'll all be."

"What about the woman?" Ace said. "I thought we was going to ransom her. After all, her daddy did own that bank we robbed in Houston. He's gotta be worth plenty 'cause we didn't take that much from him."

Cass frowned. Unfortunately, what Ace said was true. The Houston bank robbery hadn't gone as well as they'd hoped. They'd only managed to clean out the teller cages before bullets had started flying. They'd grabbed the girl as a shield and had been lucky to escape Houston with their lives. Ace had gotten rough with her a few nights later, and the hotheaded fool had almost beaten her to death with his fists. Would have if Juara hadn't stopped him.

"If we stay in Texas, we'll get caught or killed," Cass said. "It ain't worth the risk of trying to deal the girl's life for her father's money."

"Then why we been dragging her all the way from Houston?" Ace exploded.

Juara finished rolling a cigarette and poked it between his lips. "You had a pretty good time with her for a few nights until you went loco and beat her face."

Ace twisted around in his saddle. "If I wanted to hear your opinion, I'd have asked for it, greaser."

Juara had been about to strike his match, but now it fell from his fingers. He was the stronger of the two but very much aware that he could not match Ace's speed with a gun. Still, even now he was thinking about all the other ways to kill a man. Ways that this hotheaded fool of a gringo did not even suspect.

"Hold it!" Cass shouted, spurring his horse in between them. "Goddammit, we just survived the Apache! We didn't come this far to kill each other over a girl."

The two men glared at each other with hatred. Ace said, "Tell him I don't argue with Mexicans. I just kill them when they cross me."

Juara lit his cigarette. "Cass, you may tell him that I am not in the habit of beating women—even ugly ones—or killing boys. That is why he is still alive."

Cass saw an insane spark leap up into Ace's eyes, and he knew the kid was going to draw and kill Juara. Cass was damned fast with his own hands, and now he lashed out with his fist. It caught Ace on the side of his handsome face and knocked him halfway out of his saddle. By the time Ace could recover, they both had their guns drawn and cocked.

Ace stared at them. "So," he hissed, "this is how it's going to be, huh, Cass? You and the greaser against me. Is that it?"

"No," Cass said. "We might be better off to kill you but I have a feeling you'll get yourself killed and maybe take some of the heat off our backtrail doing it. Ride out of here, Ace. Take the woman and ride back the way we came."

Ace rubbed the side of his jaw. "I got a third of the bank money coming. I want it."

"No," Cass said. "You're the one that figures to use the woman as a hostage. Take her and do whatever you want. Maybe you can pull it off with a ransom, but I doubt it. At any rate, this finishes it between us."

Ace was starting to realize what kind of trouble he'd bitten off for himself. "Now wait a minute! We'd never make it back across Apache country! You know that. At least let me ride into El Paso with you. Give me a lousy hundred dollars for a hotel and food for me and the woman."

Cass and Juara exchanged glances. Juara then looked at the girl. "I would not like to see the Apache get her," he said.

"All right then," Cass decided, "that's the way we'll do it."

He reached into his saddlebags and pulled out the wad of bills they'd gotten in Houston. He counted a hundred dollars knowing there was only about six hundred left for he and Juara to use getting to California.

"Here's a hundred dollars," Cass said, "and we're doing you a favor. You just go ahead and play out that ransom thing. Maybe you'll make yourselves a fortune. At any rate, you'll have a good time with the woman if you don't use your fists on her again."

Ace counted the money. Satisfied, he said, "I can't say I'll miss either of you stiff-backed sons of bitches. I say good riddance."

"Get out of here," Cass ordered, his gun still in his fist. "But remember one thing—if you are captured by the Rangers or the sheriff, you never heard of us. Is that clear?"

Ace nodded. "Same goes both ways," he spat. "But I ain't going to get captured. I'm going to marry that woman and then tie into her father's money."

"What?"

Ace grinned broadly. "I been thinking about it a lot," he said. "And last night I told her my plans and that I'd kill her father if she said a word about me forcing her to marry."

"You're loco as hell," Juara said.

Ace's cheeks flamed. "Am I? We was wearing masks during the holdup. I'll just explain that I rescued her and we fell in love and got married before I brought her back."

Juara threw his head back and laughed, but Cass saw no sense in pushing the matter any farther. It was an insane plan. Just the kind of a crazy scheme that a kid like Ace would concoct. The kid thought he was the greatest lover of all time, that he was so damned handsome and charming he could beat a woman and still make her love or at least obey him.

"Good luck," he said. "I'd still find her a doctor."

"She'll be fine," Ace said. "She just needs food and rest like our horses."

"You'll wind up killing her," Juara said. "I better not see you in California."

"Come on!" Cass said. "Let's get out of here."

"We'll be along," Ace said, holding the lead rope attached to Gabe's horse. "And damned if we'll exchange hellos on the streets of El Paso!"

The young woman watched the other two gallop away with a sense of panic. She had loathed all three of her captors but Ace was the one she hated the most. He was the one who had beaten her senseless and who had first raped her. He was the one that she prayed to see die slowly.

"Hey listen," Ace snapped, "we'll wait until after sundown before we follow them into El Paso. That way, it'll seem that we don't know 'em. Besides, if there's any Texas Rangers waiting for us, Cass and Juara will be the ones that will have to settle."

The woman raised her chin a little higher. Her face had lost most of its puffiness but bluish marks caused by his fists still remained around her lips and eyes.

"I heard what you said to them."

"Yeah? So it's a pretty good plan, isn't it? I get your father's inheritance and you get me and the chance to live. I'd say that's a fair trade, wouldn't you?"

The woman wanted to scream at him. To tell him that he was loco, like the Mexican had said—insane. And yet . . . yet she knew that humiliating him might actually set him to beating her again and that, this time, there was no one to keep him from killing her.

"Well?" he demanded.

She could not look into his eyes. "Yeah," she said in a broken voice. "It's fair."

Ace grinned boyishly. "Damned if it isn't! By the way, what is your name?"

"Margaret."

"I'll call you Meg," he said, reaching out and pinching her cheek almost playfully. "And you'll come to love me. I promise that. Every girl I ever courted or made love to has always wanted to marry me. You're going to be a pretty lucky woman. You treat me right, Meg, I can make you a happy woman."

His hand dropped to her blouse, and she shivered with revulsion. "You understand?"

Not trusting her voice, Meg nodded.

"Good," he said. "Let's ride over to the river and find us the shade of a cottonwood tree to rest under. We could use a bath and some cleaning up before we go into town."

Meg said nothing. Ace yanked the lead rope to her horse and led off toward the Rio Grande. When he found the shade of some big trees, he tied their horses and took her arm, then pushed her down to the river's edge.

"Undress and wash," he said, pulling off his boots.

Meg hesitated until he jumped to his feet cursing. He grabbed her throat, and his thumb dug into her windpipe until she could not breathe.

"Meg," he said, his voice shaking with fury, "you still need some training, just like a puppy dog. Now you undress and do what I say or I'll grab me up a stick and whip you raw."

She wanted to defy him but could not. Slowly, numbly, she undressed until she was naked. Ace finished undressing then took her arm and pulled her down into the shallow river.

"Sit down on the sand and use it to scrub off the dirt and the sweat," he ordered.

Meg watched as he demonstrated and then did as he told her.

"Tell you one thing," he said, "a girl like you, with a banker for a father, why, I'll just bet you were never so poor you had to use sand when you ran out of soap, did you?"

"No."

"Well, I did. I come from Alabama, and I never even knew my father. He ran away with a saloon girl and left my mother and us six kids. We was so poor we had to eat bugs and stuff sometimes. People always lookin' down on us and such. We was the poorest family in the country. White trash, a man called us."

Ace gazed up at the blue sky as the water rolled over his long, slender body with its smooth muscles. "I killed that man when I was fifteen and took his six-gun and practiced with it until I was faster than any man that ever came out of my country. I outdrew a local constable and killed him, and then I went to Mississippi. Killed men there and took their women, horses, and money. I come a long way to get this far. I come from nothing, Meg—so if you don't understand me, that's why."

"I'll never understand you," she blurted. "I don't care how poor a start you got in life. It still don't give you the right to rob, kidnap, rape, and murder people."

Ace rolled over to gaze at her. "Maybe it does and maybe it don't," he said. "But I'll tell you one thing I know about life. Nobody gives a poor boy anything. He's got to take everything he gets from somebody else by force. Otherwise, he'll always be poor."

Meg swallowed nervously. She felt his hand slip across her breasts.

"I don't want to," she whispered. "Please, Ace, I don't want to!"

In answer, he twisted her arm and pulled her up on the sand. Then he fell on her like a hungry animal. Meg closed her eyes and detached her mind from her body.

"You treat me good," he said in her ear, "I'll make you happy. I'll make you happier than you ever been with a man before. And you been with men before, Meg. I can tell that."

Meg felt tears sting her eyes, and when Ace twisted her face up to his and looked down at her, his eyes were glazed with pleasure and he was smiling.

"How many men?"

"Please, I . . ."

"It was a lot of men, wasn't it?"

"A couple," she admitted.

"What were their names?"

"What . . . what does it matter?"

He wound his fingers into her hair, and his body punished her with deep strokes.

"Their names!"

"Matthew," she gasped. "The first was a boy I liked. I was only fourteen."

"And the next?"

"You're hurting me!"

He released her hair and stopped driving himself into her so roughly.

"The next?"

"Tom. He was a man. I thought I was in love, and we were going to get married."

"Did he leave you?"

"No, I left him."

"For another man?"

"Yes!" Meg panted. "I . . . oh, will you stop this!"

"You're not so high and fancy, Miss Banker's daughter! I'm gonna make you forget all the others you laid with right now."

Meg closed her eyes. If she had had a gun or a knife in her hand, she would've killed him, that was for certain.

CHAPTER FIVE

Cass and Juara found a good hotel in El Paso. They boarded their exhausted horses and had them grained and reshod. At the Casino House, they bought a bottle of whiskey, had a bath, and ordered a Chinaman to pick up their clothes at their room after they'd had a dinner of steaks and potatoes. That evening, as they sat in their hotel room and shared the bottle, they talked about their plans.

"We'll wait two days," Cass said, "and then we'll hit a bank in this town and clear out fast."

Juara looked surprised. "Maybe it would be better to wait. We're already in enough trouble in this state."

"That's why we ought to rob a Texas bank and go into hiding down in Old Mexico where you got some friends that wouldn't mind earning a little money protecting us for a while until things cool down," Cass said. "After a few weeks, we can ride on to California."

But Juara was not completely reassured. "Maybe the same thing that happened to us at that bank in Houston might happen again."

"No," Cass said with confidence. "We made some mistakes in Houston and almost paid for them with our lives. But Ace was part of the problem. We never knew what he was going to do next."

"We should kill him," Juara spat angrily. "If he talks . . ."

"He won't talk," Cass said. "And even if he gets shot and confesses with his dying breath, what do we care? By then, we'll be living the life of rich cattle ranchers in California."

"This land your brother bought ten years ago and left you in his will," Juara said. "Where is it again?"

"Near a place called Modesto," Cass told him. "It is warm in the summer and the winter, and they grow everything. The sky is always sunny. No more snow and blizzards for us."

Juara smiled. "Tell me again about all the beautiful señoritas in this place called Modesto."

"They are everywhere," Cass said. "I visited my brother just three years ago and the women were very beautiful. They are looking for strong, handsome men like us. Men with money in their pockets."

Juara chuckled. "I like the sound of this very much. But after Houston, I am not sure about a bank. Perhaps it would be better to rob a stagecoach or even some men in this town."

"No," Cass said. "We need one big stake before we leave Texas. Tomorrow morning we'll look over the town, choose a bank and rob it tomorrow afternoon.

"But our horses, they are not ready."

Cass frowned. "All right, then we'll sell 'em and buy fresh ones, the fastest and strongest that can be bought in El Paso. We'll have them ready and waiting behind the bank."

"It is a good plan," Juara conceded. "But I wish we were going to rob a stagecoach instead. And I would like to kill Ace before we leave and take that woman with us."

"No," Cass said firmly as he took a long pull of whiskey. "She's big trouble. Her father would hire bounty hunters to track us down all the way to the end of the earth if he don't get her back. Let Ace enjoy her while he can. She'll be the cause of his downfall. Mark my words."

Juara scowled and reached for the bottle. "I guess you are right," he said, "but that was a pretty good-looking woman before Ace beat the hell out of her. I would liked to have tried a little of that."

"Save it for the California señoritas," Cass told him. "You'll be glad you did."

Juara chuckled. "I never asked, señor, but how did your brother die so young? A bullet? Whiskey? What?"

"He fucked himself to death," Cass deadpanned. "Just like you and I will probably do when we get to Modesto."

They both laughed then, and late that night, they fell asleep half drunk but very happy.

In the morning, they had aching heads and cotton mouths but after a huge breakfast and plenty of coffee, they felt well enough to survey the border town's three thriving banks. The biggest was the El Paso Bank, but it had a shotgun guard waiting inside and another stationed near the vault, so they chose the Bank of Texas, a small but prosperous-looking bank that seemed to have no guards and plenty of wealthy-looking customers.

"We will come in just before closing time, locking the doors and shuttering the windows as soon as we pull our guns and get everyone out in the lobby," Cass said under his breath as they headed for the livery. "If there are any customers inside, we'll rob them, too. If we can get into the vault, we ought to get away with thousands. And even if we can't, the teller cages will be crammed with cash. Several thousand at least by the end of the day's business."

"And the horses? Will we just tie them behind the bank?" Juara asked in a worried voice. "What if that makes someone suspicious?"

"We take that chance with only the two of us. If Ace were with us, I'd have him stay with the horses. But we'll do all right. If it goes smooth—and we don't have to use our guns—we'll only be inside about five minutes. We'll bring a sack of ropes and gags, and one of us can tie up the people inside while the other stuffs money into the empty sack. It'll work."

"I hope so," Juara said, stroking his black mustache as he watched a pretty woman move across the street. "To die so young would leave so many women weeping for me, it would be a sad thing."

Cass just shook his head. He liked the big Mexican and enjoyed their bantering and boasting. But the thing of it was, his own boasting was made in jest while Juara, like Ace, actually believed he was a great and irresistible lover.

At the stable, they quickly made a deal for a pair of fine horses in exchange for their worn down ones. It cost them an extra fifty dollars, but both men were satisfied and when the fresh horses were saddled and mounted, the liveryman said, "I thought you boys were going to stick around El Paso for a few weeks."

"Changed our mind," Cass said. "Got restless feet."

"Mighty restless considering you stayed only one day," the man said. "Where you heading next?"

"Denver," Cass said quickly. "We're riding north to Denver."

"Guess that's a big town," the man said. "Never been there myself. But at least you got the horses to get to Colorado in a hurry."

"That we do," Cass said as he winked and rode his horse away with Juara riding beside him.

That afternoon at 4:45, they tied their horses between the bank and Bill Hawkin's General Store.

"Hey kid!"

A ragged boy of about fourteen turned to look at them. "Yeah?"

"You want to earn four bits?" Cass asked him with a broad smile.

"Why sure!"

"Then hold our horses while we go to the bank for a minute."

The boy thought that was a fine idea. "Nice horses," he said, taking their reins.

"Yes, they are," Cass said. "That's why we don't want to leave them here untended."

The boy nodded with understanding. He looked at the Winchesters stuffed into the rifle boots. "Good looking rifles, too."

"Yeah," Cass said, paying him a quarter. "You get half now, half when we get back. Understand?"

"Sure, Mister. You both take your time."

Juara hitched up his gunbelt. "You better be here when we get back," he warned.

"Yes, sir!"

Satisfied, they left the horses in his care and entered the bank. There were three customers, two women and a man, all of them old and prosperous-looking. As Cass had instructed, Juara backed up to the door, then locked it and drew his gun.

Cass drew his gun beside the bank teller's cage. He grabbed one of the old women and yelled, "This is a holdup! Everyone freeze!"

The women screamed. The old man bolted for the door and Juara flattened him with a vicious uppercut to the jaw that knocked him skidding back across the polished mahogany floor.

"I said freeze!" Cass shouted again, as the bank manager started to open his desk drawer.

Cass pointed his gun at the man. "I won't miss from this range. Unless you want to die, you'd better get over there and open that vault."

The bank manager, a pale and ascetic-looking man with wire-rimmed glasses and fluttering fingers, popped to his feet and rushed over to the vault.

"It's not even locked! Don't shoot anybody, for God's sakes!"

"Juara! The sack!"

Juara emptied the sack of rope and gags they'd made from their hotel bed sheets. He tossed the sack to Cass and grabbed one of the screaming women, shoving a gag down her throat. When she began to choke and claw at his face, Juara drew his pistol and whipped her across the head. The woman went limp, but he lowered her to the floor and pulled her dress down neatly around her ankles.

"Anybody else want to cause us trouble?" Cass asked. "If not, tellers, empty your cages and put your money on the counter."

There were three tellers, all young men, and they acted quickly. Cass hurried around the counter and jumped into the vault.

"Jackpot!" he whispered as he bumped into the bank manager who was cradling a pile of cash in his arms. The cash spilled all over the floor.

"Here," Cass said as the bank manager dropped to his knees and began scooping it up. "I'll even help you put it in this sack."

"Thank you, sir!" the man stammered.

Five minutes later, they had also stuffed the money from the cages into the bulging sack and were about to finish binding and gagging the last of the bank tellers when there was a loud knocking at the front door.

Cass looked up and saw another old woman staring myopically through the window at them. She looked upset.

"You were supposed to pull the curtains!"

Juara jumped to his feet. "Well, what do we do now? She can't figure out what is going on in here."

Cass swore silently. "Let her in before she brings the whole town on the run," he said with exasperation. "Let her in!"

Juara yanked open the door and the angry old woman stomped inside.

"Mildred," she cried, "what on earth are you doing sleeping on the floor? I've been waiting . . . oh my Gawd!"

The old lady swayed around in a full circle and then made a beeline for the front door, screeching like a scalded cat.

"Let's get out of here!" Cass shouted, picking up the sack and racing for the door.

Juara was right behind him. At the instant they burst out of the bank, all eyes and attention were on the lady, but when they hit the boardwalk, someone shouted, "The bank's been robbed! There they are!"

Cass and Juara ducked into the alley and, to their horror and amazement, their horses were gone.

"Son of a bitch!" Cass bellowed. "I'll kill that kid!"

Juara had the same intention. A gun banged out on the street and, since there was no going back, they raced down the alley and followed the tracks of their horses.

"There!" Juara shouted, already puffing and out of breath. "Behind that building!"

They rounded a building and saw the kid and their horses. He was on foot, pulling the two saddled animals along behind himself.

"Hey!" Cass yelled, raising his gun. "Stop or I'll shoot!"

The kid was too afraid to stop. He kept running so Cass fired and then so did Juara. The kid seemed to break apart, and when he hit the dirt, he began to twitch as if caught in some giant spasm. Cass and Juara raced on and managed to catch their horses.

"Help," the boy cried weakly.

"You got what you deserve, you little bastard!" Cass shouted, holstering his gun and swinging into the saddle.

Juara hesitated for a moment, his gun held just inches from the boy's face. He watched the boy's eyes dilate with terror and then, on a whim, he decided to spare the kid because, had he been in the same circumstances, he'd have guessed a bank robbery and tried to steal the horses, too.

Juara mounted as gunfire began to bracket the alley. He reined his horse after Cass who had the money and used his spurs hard. Minutes later, they burst out of the end of the alley racing for the Rio Grande and the safety of Old Mexico.

When the shooting started, Ace jumped out of bed, grabbing his six-gun. He rushed to the window and looked down in the street to see men racing around in confusion. He could hear shouting, but there was so much noise it took him a few moments to realize the bank had been robbed. Ace saw a sheriff come bustling into the crowd, calling for volunteers to form a posse to chase after the bank robbers.

Suddenly, a woman shrieked and everyone rushed into the alley. A few moments later, Ace saw a kid being rushed across the street toward the doctor's office. Ace saw the blood on the boy's shirt and the deathly pale color of his face.

"What happened?" Meg asked, getting out of bed.

Ace let the curtains slip from his hand. "Bank robbery. Some kid was shot and taken to the doctor's office. He didn't look too good."

Meg's hand flew to her mouth. "Was it Cass and Juara?"

"Most likely," Ace said, coming over to the bed and slumping down on it to consider how this would affect him. "I'll find out soon enough."

"Well, what are you going to do?"

Ace stood up and began to pace back and forth. "I don't know," he said. "I got to find out more and then decide." He stopped pacing and grabbed a pillow, then ripped its case. "I've gotta tie and gag you until I get back," he said.

"No," she whispered. "Please don't. I'll stay here and be quiet. I swear I will."

"I can't trust you—not yet," he told her. "Now do as I say. Open your mouth."

Meg opened her mouth, and the gag was pulled tight. She was pushed back across the bed, and her hands and feet were quickly tied. She felt like a plucked chicken waiting to be slaughtered as she lay naked on the bed. He patted her behind affectionately.

"Don't worry," he said. "I wouldn't leave this unless I had to. Besides, you're my key to the good life." A moment later, the door slammed shut, and she heard it lock.

Meg did not try to struggle but lay still, waiting for Ace to return. He returned just fifteen minutes later, untied her, and removed the gag.

"It was them all right. The posse rode out just now with two Texas Rangers, the sheriff, and his deputies along with about twenty men. They're madder than hell. Bank lost over ten thousand dollars but what really got 'em upset was the shooting of the boy. He'll live, but he's in for a long hard row of it. Seems he tried to steal their horses. Been me, I'd have killed the little bastard."

Meg swallowed nervously. "What are we going to do now?"

Ace grinned. "I'm coming back to bed with you, honey. And if the posse ain't back by ten o'clock tomorrow morning, I reckon you're going to help me rob the El Paso Bank."

"No!"

Ace jumped on her and kissed her roughly. "Don't ever say no to me, Meg! Never!"

"But . . . but please. Not a bank. We could get killed! If we get married, my father would help you turn honest. I know he would. You could have me and a good life. You don't need to rob a bank anymore!"

Ace climbed off of her. "I guess I don't at that," he said. "But then again, your father might not be as grateful to see you as I first thought. And maybe he'd even like to see me swing by a rope for robbing his big old bank." Ace winked. "So I'm asking myself, who needs Houston and your father? We can do it all on our own. Maybe even do it both ways. What do you think?"

Meg looked up at him. "I think you're making the biggest mistake of your life, Ace. I think you're pushing your luck way too far."

He looked down at her and laughed, sounding wild and crazy. For a moment, she thought he was going to hurt her, but then he unbuckled his gunbelt and started to undress.

"What I like most about you, besides the way you make love, is that you're real honest with me. Real honest."

"I . . . I just don't see any reason for us to rob a bank. Not when my father will help us."

Ace finished removing his clothes. "The thing of it is," he said, "something in me just won't let Cass and that greaser do me one better and get rich quick while I have to kiss your father's fat ass. So if I rob a bigger and richer bank than they did—and use them to draw off the law while I'm doing it—then that's one better on them. I like that idea too damn much to let it pass. You understand what I'm sayin'?"

She shook her head.

He climbed onto her and smiled. "It don't matter, honey. Tomorrow morning when we waltz into that bank and waltz out with more money than even your father has seen, we'll have the last laugh on everyone. We'll be rich and free, and we won't go back to Houston, that's for damn sure."

"Where will we go?" she asked, taking him inside of her.

"Maybe to a place called Modesto, California," he whispered. "Where the sun always shines, the señoritas smile at every man, and things grow year around."

Meg wrapped her arms and her legs around him and held him with all of her strength. She hated herself but what choice did she have? She had to survive.

CHAPTER SIX

Just sixty miles south of El Paso along the Rio Grande, Gabe knew he had a serious Indian problem. From the looks of the half dozen Apache who blocked his trail, Gabe was sure that, if he made the wrong decision, he'd be dead in less than fifteen minutes.

Ever since leaving Langtry on one of Judge Roy Bean's "best" horses, Gabe had been cussing and fuming because the judge's horse wasn't worth a damn. In fact, Gabe figured he'd have done a whole lot better if he'd attempted to reach El Paso on Old Buck because the dun gelding he rode was not sound. The animal had gone lame about two days after Gabe had started on the outlaws' trail, and he'd been afoot ever since leading the damned thing.

Gabe's own feet were sore, and because he'd not been able to make much time, he knew that he was falling farther and farther behind the men and the woman he was chasing. And now, to top it all off, he had run smack into a tough group of renegade Apache that looked like they were about to attack. The decision was simple, Gabe thought. Since I have no hope of outrunning them, I either try and negotiate for my life, or I fight for it. Gabe's gut reaction was to fight, but because he was at heart an Indian and knew why they hated the white men, he decided that he would attempt a negotiation.

Gabe raised his hand up and palm out in the universal peace sign used by all the Plains Indians and northern frontiersmen. The Apache, seated on runty scrub ponies some hundred yards away, did not respond but at least they had not started firing.

"Peace, brothers," Gabe called in Oglala Sioux and then in the language of the Cheyenne.

Still the Apache did not respond except to look toward the man in the center of their attack line, the one that Gabe knew was their leader.

Gabe waited patiently. He hoped that the six-gun and the Winchester that Judge Roy Bean had loaned him would be more reliable than his damned horse. If they were, maybe he could kill three or four of the Apache before they could reach him, and then pick the rest off if they still had the urge to fight.

"I am a brother to the Indian," Gabe called in Oglala as his big hands moved in sign language. "I have no wish to kill my brothers."

The Apache listened and then began to argue among themselves. Gabe waited with the hot sun blazing in the sky and salty perspiration burning his eyes. Finally, after about twenty minutes of arguing, the leader of the Apache raised his hand in peace, and Gabe expelled a deep sigh of relief.

The Apache moved forward on their tough little ponies, and the Winchester cradled in the crook of Gabe's left arm did not move an inch.

"You speak white man talk," the Apache leader grunted, reining his pony to a halt no less than thirty feet from Gabe.

"I do."

"How you call yourself brother to Indian, gray eyes?"

Gabe slowly reached behind his saddle and untied his buffalo vest with his mother's Sioux painting.

"I was raised by the Oglala," he said, his eyes fixed on the leader. "My Oglala name is Long Rider. It was given to me because I once rode many days to save my people. My father was Little Wound, a great warrior, and his brother was the great chief Red Cloud. Like you and your brothers, I recognize the wisdom of Wakan-tanka, the Great Spirit. I am at peace with Mother Earth, and I do not fear death."

The leader was silent for a full minute. He wore a bow, and a quiver was strung over his back, though he also carried an old Army Colt slung from his saddle horn. To everyone's surprise, he removed his bow and quiver, dismounted, and approached Long Rider.

"If what you say is true, then shoot something like an Oglala."

Long Rider dropped his reins. The dun wasn't fit to run away. He took the bow and selected an arrow, then slowly pivoted toward a stand of cottonwood trees.

"The littlest one," he said, pointing with his long, crooked right index finger.

The Apache followed his meaning and were impressed. The thin young tree was no bigger around than a woman's wrist, and it was at least forty yards distant. Gabe nocked the arrow and wished he had a good Oglala bow and arrow instead of this short, stiff Apache one. But the arrow was very straight and the feathers on it were good so he felt confident as he drew the bowstring back to his ear. As a boy, he had learned to kill rabbits and sometimes even quail in flight with his own bow and arrow.

When he released, the arrow leapt from his bowstring and streaked across the distance right on target. The head of the arrow bit deeply into the cottonwood, and the shaft quivered like dog on the scent of a hare. When Long Rider respectfully returned the Apache's bow, he could see that he had made a good impression. There were probably men among them that had not used those traditional Indian weapons for many years and could not have duplicated his shooting.

"I believe you now," the Apache said. "But why do you walk so far when you have a horse to ride?"

"He is lame," Long Rider explained. "He looks good but is no good. Bad legs."

The Apache grunted with understanding. "Then we will feast on him now."

Gabe knew better than to object. The Apache were thin and hungry-looking. As soon as he unsaddled and removed his bit and bridle, one Apache shot the dun, and then two more fell upon it with their knives while the others quickly gathered firewood. The Apache ate the dun half raw, with blood running out of the corners of their mouths and down their forearms as they wolfed the seared meat down. Long Rider had no qualms about what they were doing. He, like most Indians, had often eaten dog and to him, a horse was no different. It was an animal to be used until it had no use except to feed the Indian.

Later, around the camp fire, the Apache were very curious to know more about Long Rider's curious past. A white man with a red man's heart and mind intrigued them. They listened carefully as he answered their questions.

"It is no good to fight the white man and all of his armies," he told them.

"What about Sitting Bull and his warriors?" the leader asked. "They fought and won."

"No," Gabe said quietly. "They might have killed the soldiers that day at Little Big Horn, but they were wise enough to understand that the white people would rise up against them and kill them all if they remained on their own lands. So they all fled. Many to a place called Canada which is cold and where many of The People starved. Finally, they returned to the reservations. Some were taken before the army courts and sentenced to die, others were killed. It was bad."

The Apache stared into their camp fire. "We will fight," the leader, whose name was Blue Horse said. "We will fight until the end because there is no other way."

"There is always a way. You must try to find peace. I know it is hard because a warrior asks the Great Spirit to die in battle with honor. But there are the women and the children to think about. They deserve to live, and they need the warrior to protect them, even on the white man's reservations."

"Many of us have died already," an Apache said. "Six days ago, two of our warriors were killed by three men with a woman."

Gabe listened attentively. "They also tried to kill me. You can still see the marks they left on my face. I am going to find and kill them."

"Then I will give you our best horse," the Apache leader said.

"Many thanks," Long Rider told the Apache before he went to his saddle blankets and found much-needed sleep. That night, Long Rider slept soundly and without fear. The Apache might torture an enemy, but they would never betray a friend.

He awoke at first light and declined to feast again as the Apache were preparing to do. Thanking them once more, he saddled the horse they brought out to him and pushed on toward El Paso.

When Gabe approached the hot and dusty border town

late that night, he chose to sleep the morning hours down near the Rio Grande. When dawn peeked over the eastern hills, Gabe silently rode into El Paso and began to visit each of the liveries, searching for his sorrel gelding whose presence would tell him that the men and the woman he sought were still in Texas.

But by eight o'clock, he learned that there had been not one, but two bank robberies on two consecutive days earlier in the week.

"First one, they got away with ten thousand and gunned down a kid that was trying to prevent their escape by taking their horses," a grizzled old stable master growled, spitting tobacco juice into the dirt. "Second one happened just the next morning when the sheriff, the Texas Rangers, and everybody else who could ride and shoot were out chasing the first bunch."

"Describe the bank robbers," Gabe said, unsaddling the Indian pony and leading it into a corral where it immediately attacked several of the other horses and established its dominance despite the fact that it was the smallest horse in the bunch.

"Mean little pony you got there," the stable man commented. "Where the hell did you get him?"

"The Apache gave him to me," Gabe said.

The stable man chuckled. "Sure they did! Probably threw in a few souvenir scalps and arrowheads, too!"

"Describe the bank robbers."

"The pair that robbed the Bank of Texas were damned ugly. Big Mexican and a weasel-faced son of a bitch about six-foot-four."

"Cass and Juara," Gabe said. "What about the second bank robbery?"

The stable man spat again. "Well, that's the funny one, all right. Nobody quite knows what the hell happened there.

You see, a man went into the El Paso Bank the next morning and walked out with about thirty thousand dollars. Hell, it's the biggest bank in town and, like I said, the law was out chasin' down the other two."

"Go on."

"Well, this dandy gets all the loot and races out around the back and then gets away."

"What's so funny about that?"

"Well, they found a woman lying in the alley. She'd been pistol-whipped by the bank robber and knocked out cold. Everybody that went back to see her done wiped out the tracks so that the sheriff couldn't figure out what happened. But they say this woman was with the bank robber and had been holding their horses."

"That doesn't make any sense at all."

" 'Course it don't!" the stable man swore. "But something fishy was going on between her and the bank robber. The sheriff has his back up and swears that he'll keep her locked in his jail cell until she confesses everything."

Gabe shook his head in bewilderment. "Was she a pretty young woman with long brown hair and soft brown eyes?"

"That's right! How'd you know?"

"I met the bunch of them once," Gabe said. "Down near Langtry."

"In Judge Roy Bean's country?"

"That's right."

The stable man scoffed. "I'd a figured that ornery old coot would have drank himself to death if someone hadn't already shot him for being so crooked and makin' up all those fines."

"He's still alive."

"Well, mister, you are lucky to have got out of Langtry with the shirt on your back. Judge Bean, he must be getting more charitable in his old age."

Gabe figured there was no sense in sticking around town, but since he'd just paid a day's board bill on the skinny Apache pony and his own stomach was growling, he guessed he'd go see the young woman that was being held in jail. Maybe she'd know where those three no-good bastards were headed.

The sheriff of El Paso was in a cantankerous mood when Gabe intercepted him outside his office.

"Listen, mister," he said, jabbing the point of his finger into Gabe's chest. "You're either going to tell me what you want to talk to her about, or I'm going to run you the hell out of my town right now!"

Gabe snubbed down his own anger. "All right," he said. "I'm from Houston, and I knew her as a friend. Maybe I can get her to talk a little."

"Is that where she's from? Hell, neither me nor the Texas Rangers who have been interrogating her have been able to get that much information. She looks all buttery and cries at the damn drop of a hat, but that woman is tough!"

"Let me talk to her in private," Gabe said. "You've got nothing to lose."

"Maybe nothing to gain, either," the sheriff groused. "How do I know I can trust you to tell us what she said?"

"You can't," Gabe admitted, "but since you're not learning anything anyway, what's to lose?"

The sheriff chewed at the tip of his handlebar mustache. His face was dark with worry. "Between the two bank robberies, we lost nearly forty thousand dollars from this town. That's a hell of a blow for a place this size. A lot of people are going to be in big trouble if we don't recover the money."

"I thought the law said that banks were required to be insured with the federal government for this sort of thing," Gabe said.

"Yeah, well, that might be so, but nobody seems to be coming to town with a suitcase of cash to replace what's been stolen!"

"What about the trail of the robbers?"

"They were damn smart that way, too. We lost 'em in some rocky country. We heard that they were on their way to Denver, so the Texas Rangers are following up on that end of things. I personally think the first two men went into Mexico to hide. But of course, it's the young dandy that we're all most interested in catching. He's the one with nearly thirty thousand dollars in cash. I sure can't figure why the girl would want to protect him since he pistol-whipped her."

"That's one of the first questions I'll ask her myself," Gabe said, "if you'll let me talk to her in private."

The sheriff chewed faster on his mustache. He was a man in his thirties, handsome but very grim and humorless.

"Okay," he said finally. "You got fifteen minutes. I'll clear my office. As soon as you're done, I want you to meet me across the street. If you try to run out, we'll come after you with orders to kill. Savvy?"

"I sure do," Gabe said. "You couldn't make it any plainer if you tried."

"All right, then let's go on inside."

A few minutes later, Gabe was standing alone in front of the cell looking through the bars at the girl.

"I guess you must not remember me," he said. "You were running a fever when those three men brought you into my camp at night. I thought you might die."

Meg looked at the tall man with the lingering purple bruises on his face. "I remember you," she said. "You were kind to me. I thought they killed you for sure."

"So did they," Gabe said. "But like a bad dream, I'm gonna keep comin' back to them until they either kill me or I kill them. But for that to happen, I'm going to need your help."

Meg smiled bitterly. "As you can plainly see, I'm in no position to help you or anyone else. They are trying to send me to prison."

"Maybe we could make a deal with them," Gabe said. "Anything is better than just clamming up and going to prison."

She shook her head. "The truth of the matter is, I deserve worse than prison; I deserve to rot in hell. You see, mister, I helped Ace rob the El Paso Bank."

"Why?"

"I was afraid he'd kill me otherwise."

"Did you tell the sheriff that?" Gabe asked.

"I was too ashamed of . . . of what he did to me," Meg said. "And now, look at the mess I'm in. I can never go back home, and I can't stay here. I can't clear my name, and I feel like a stupid whore."

"You can change things some," Gabe said quietly. "You can tell me what happened after they left me for dead. Why did they split up?"

In a very few words, Meg told Gabe about the friction between the three outlaws and how Ace and Juara had almost got into a fight.

"Where did they go?"

"Mexico, I think," Meg said, "but only until the heat was off. Cass inherited some big ranch near a place called Modesto, California. He talked about it all the time. Got so both Juara and Ace believed all his stories about señoritas and such. I think that's where Ace was heading. I think he was following Cass and Juara to Modesto. He was going to show them that he could get an even bigger bank haul than they'd gotten the day before."

"Those are crazy reasons for Ace to want to go all

the way to California," Gabe said, only half believing her story.

"Maybe so," she said, "but Ace is crazy."

Gabe squeezed the bars to her jail cell. "Why don't you just tell the sheriff and those Texas Rangers what you just told me?"

"If I tell them the truth, they'll get hold of my father and mother in Houston, and they'll never forgive me. They'd be shamed and looked down upon for having such a stupid slut of a daughter."

"Don't be so rough on yourself," Gabe said. "It's him that's bad, not you."

"Mister, can you try and get me out of here?"

"Way I hear it," Gabe said, "you tried to stop Ace and that's why he pistol-whipped you. Is that true?"

Her eyes dropped to the cell floor and she nodded.

"You're not an accomplice, you're a victim," Gabe said. "I'd let you go free in a minute."

"Talk to the sheriff," Meg pleaded. "Tell him that I promise to lead you to where they were going, but only if we go together."

"But you already told me they were going to Modesto."

She swallowed. "I can help you. I know where they are going, and I swear that I'll take you there if you can get me out of here. Consider that I come from a pretty wealthy family in Houston. If I can clear my name, help recover the money and everything, then I can go home with my head up and not be disowned. I'm used to money, but they'll turn their backs on me if I don't come through and make things right. So I have to keep my promise to you, or I'll lose my family's love and my inheritance."

"All right, I'll talk to the sheriff," Gabe said.

"And you won't tell him where they're going?"

"Nope. If I did that, he might want to go himself or at

least send some Pinkerton men or something. I mean to catch those three men by myself and settle the score."

"So do I," Meg vowed. She got up and came over to the bars. Up close, Gabe could see that she was getting prettier every moment and that the effects of her earlier beatings were almost gone now.

"Mister, if you get me out of here and take me to California, I swear you'll have no regrets—from the first night to our last."

Gabe felt his cheeks warm. "I guess that I'd better speak to the sheriff right now."

She reached through the bars and touched his face. "You and me," she whispered, "we have a lot in common, you know. We have the same purposes in mind."

CHAPTER SEVEN

"Absolutely Goddamn not!" the sheriff stormed the moment Gabe asked him to release the young woman from his custody. "I got a United States marshal coming into town on the stage tomorrow. She'll either cooperate with him or else be taken before a court of law and sentenced to a long prison term."

"And by then," Gabe said with exasperation, "any chance we might have of recovering the money will be gone."

"What's this 'we' crap?" the sheriff demanded, his eyes narrowing suspiciously. "You lookin' to make yourself some reward money? Because if that's your plan, you can forget all about it. Just tell me everything the girl said and then be on your way."

Gabe did not appreciate the man's attitude, but he was accustomed to this kind of reaction. Frontier lawmen were typically the kind of men who made the rules and never bent them to meet exceptions. Maybe that was the way they had to operate to stay alive because if you didn't draw the line someplace, someone was going to try and cross it.

"Sorry you feel the way you do," Gabe said. "I would have thought that, since you had no leads and no idea where the bank robbers went, you'd be willing to try most anything rather than sit around here stewing over the mess you're in."

"We're not just stewing!" the sheriff snapped. "I told you that the marshal is coming to take her to Austin. She'll talk to him, I'll bet."

Gabe figured there was nothing more to be gained with this man so he turned to walk away. But the sheriff grabbed his arm and tried to jerk him around.

"Hey," the man growled, "where the hell do you think you're going? I'm not finished with you yet."

Gabe yanked his arm away. "As far as I'm concerned, you are."

"What did she say in there?"

"Just what I told you. She wants me to help her find the man that pistol-whipped her in the alley so she can clear her name and recover the money."

"If anyone takes her, I'll be that man," the sheriff said. "And if you ain't telling me everything she said, then I just might jail you."

"On what charges?"

"Withholding information of importance in the commission of a bank robbery! How does that sound?"

"Sounds like something you made up."

The sheriff's face darkened. "Well, I'm no lawyer, but I can find one in a hurry, and you can bet he'll come up with a charge that will stick. At the least, you'll wind up spending a month or two in jail, and mister, if I want to make you a skinny son of a bitch, I will."

Gabe felt a hard ball of ice forming in his gut. It was becoming clear that this man was ruthless and not at all adverse to bending the law to fulfill his own purposes. But right now, he was holding the aces and Gabe the losing hand.

"All right," Gabe said, "the girl told me that the man she was with was heading for Denver."

"I knew it!" The sheriff smiled confidently. "If that's the case, then the Texas Rangers probably have already apprehended the son of a bitch. What about the first pair?"

"She didn't know. Maybe Mexico, like you thought."

The sheriff frowned. "What else can you tell me?"

"That's all. She wasn't all that cooperative with me either, though she asked if I'd come back to visit her every day."

"Hmmm," the sheriff mused. "Sounds like she might be willing to trust you. Tell you what, why don't you come back tomorrow and visit her again? Maybe by then she'll be ready to tell you something more."

"I could try," Gabe said.

The sheriff jabbed Gabe in the chest again with a forefinger. "You make a point of it, stranger."

Gabe stifled an impulse to break the man's finger. "I'll try," he managed to say as he turned and headed down the street.

Late that night, Gabe brought his tough Apache pony and a second horse up the street and tied them in front of the sheriff's office. He rechecked the cinches of both animals then walked over to the door and banged on it loudly.

"Deputy!" he hollered. "Deputy, open up in there. A man has been shot in the Delta Saloon!"

Gabe drew his six-gun, reversed his grip on it, and flattened against the wall. He heard a grunt and then swearing as whoever was on duty fumbled around in the office. A light came on through the window, and when the door opened, a man in long johns with a gun in his fist stood half asleep in the empty doorway.

"What the—"

Gabe's pistol came crashing down against the deputy's

skull, and before the man could strike the porch, Gabe caught him and pulled him inside, then quickly closed the door.

Meg was on her feet and hanging onto the cell bars. "You didn't leave me!" she cried.

"Nope," he grunted, "but the thought did enter my mind a couple of hundred times since I saw you earlier. Where do they keep the keys?"

Meg squirmed. "Mister, I hate to tell you this, but the sheriff is the only one that has them."

"What?"

"That's right."

"Well . . . well what if the place caught on fire and he was gone?"

Meg shrugged. "I don't know. They even slide my food under the bars. I'm sorry."

Gabe scowled. "Not as sorry as I am," he said. "And the sheriff said that there's a United States marshal coming in on tomorrow's stage. I got a hunch I either get you out now or never."

"But how?"

Gabe came over and inspected the lock in the cell door. He rattled the door and studied it for a moment before he said, "I can either get some blacksmith tools and try and jimmy this door open, or I can go find the sheriff and try and take the keys from his person."

"Neither sounds very promising, does it?"

"Nope," Gabe said. "Or I just walk away and forget this whole mess and take my chances that you were telling the truth when you said they were all heading for this place called Modesto."

"If you do that," she said, "you'll be making a long trip west for nothing. Do you really think I'd tell you the only thing that would get me free?"

"I just don't know," Gabe said, "but I do know that I had better find those three men before anyone else does, or Judge Roy Bean is going to be sending men after me. He appears to be a vindictive son of a gun if I ever saw one."

"Well," Meg said, "it seems you are in quite a spot. So what are you going to do now?"

"Do you have any idea where the sheriff lives?"

"As a matter of fact, I do. He lives over on Olive Street. I heard him say that he just had his house painted white and brown a few weeks ago, and it's already starting to peel."

"Don't surprise me none in this sun-busted country," Gabe said. "I guess I'll go find him."

"He isn't going to give you those keys without a fight, I can tell you that."

"Life is a fight," Gabe said as he gagged the deputy and used the man's own belt to hog-tie him.

"Hurry back," Meg called sweetly. "The night is getting old."

Gabe hurried outside, and it took him twenty minutes to find the house, and even then he wasn't too sure it was the right one. He hopped over a fence and sneaked around to the back door. It was locked, so he used his knife to chisel away enough wood to pry it open. Then he entered the kitchen. Being raised by the Oglala and wearing moccasins gave him some advantage in the darkness, and since the house was small, he had no trouble sneaking into the bedroom where he found the sheriff asleep with a woman that was probably his wife.

Gabe tiptoed over to the man's coat and pants that were hanging on the bedpost and rifled the sheriff's pockets. He breathed a sigh of relief when he found the keys. Trouble was, they jingled when he removed them, and the woman started and woke up for a minute, but Gabe was already slipping out of the room and back out the kitchen door.

Five minutes later, he was opening the cell. He dragged the semiconscious deputy inside and locked the cell, then dropped the keys into his own pockets.

"Getting this man out will take some doing unless the sheriff was smart enough to keep an extra set of keys," Gabe said.

"He's going to be killing mad," Meg said. "And it won't be hard to figure out it was you that did this."

"I know," Gabe said, "but if the unreasonable so-and-so hadn't kept poking me in the chest and had acted halfway civil, then I wouldn't have put him in such an embarrassing mess."

Taking Meg by the hand, Gabe led her to the front door, where he surveyed the street. Satisfied that it was clear, he pulled her after him and they rushed outside and around to the horses.

In another ten minutes they were galloping their horses across the Rio Grande into Mexico. Gabe wasn't sure where they were going first, but he figured that Cass and Juara just might be still holed up in this rough border town. And if they were, Gabe knew that he was going to find them and try to either bust their heads and bring them back to Judge Roy Bean alive, or he was going to kill them.

It would be their choice and a far better deal than they'd given him when they'd kicked his head damn near off his shoulders.

CHAPTER EIGHT

Juárez was a rough town, squalid, dusty, and a haven for banditos as well as Americans who sought to escape the noose. As Gabe and Meg rode through the streets, they were looking for both Cass and Juara, not really expecting to see them out in the open, but not completely discounting the possibility either.

"Do you speak any Spanish?" Gabe asked.

"*Poco*," she said. "A little. Darn little. And you?"

"About the same," Gabe said, as they stopped before a small whitewashed adobe hotel and cantina. "That'll make it a lot more difficult to ask questions and get answers about Cass and Juara."

"From what I hear, it won't make much difference. Juárez depends on American money, and the cantinas are supposed to be full of cowboys on Saturday nights spending their money. I think that most of the people down here will speak at least a little English."

"That would help," Gabe said as he dismounted.

Meg also climbed down from her horse. "Do you think that the sheriff and that United States marshal will come looking for us down here?"

"It wouldn't surprise me," Gabe said. "Funny, isn't it?

We're looking for three killers, and the law is looking for them—as well as us."

"Let's just hope we all don't meet in the same place at the same time," Meg said drily.

They tied their horses up and went inside. The cantina was almost empty at this hour of the morning, and the bartender also served as the hotel keeper.

"Ah," he exclaimed when they walked in, "Señor, señorita! Welcome! Cerveza or tequila?"

"A room, *por favor.*"

"Twenty pesos, señor."

Gabe did not have any pesos. "All I have is a silver dollar," he said, taking it out of his pocket.

"Gracias, señor!" The man led them over to a table, then disappeared into a room behind his bar.

"What is he up to?" Gabe asked.

"I don't know. But I think the silver dollar was worth a lot more than twenty pesos," Meg said.

Ten minutes later, her assessment proved to be correct because the hotel keeper came rushing out leading two fat but smiling women laden with trays of hot beans, rice, and tortillas. Gabe and Meg were served beer, and when they indicated again that they did not wish to drink it, they were brought fresh milk. The meal was delicious, and they both discovered that they were famished. Afterward, they were shown to a small but clean room with a single bed and a bookcase which was supposed to double as a dresser. Finally, one of the Mexican women who had served them brought in a cracked vase filled with flowers, while another dragged in a tub and began to fill it with steaming buckets of water. When they were alone, Gabe just shook his head. "A silver dollar goes a long way in Mexico, doesn't it?"

"Apparently so," Meg said, eyeing the tub, the soft cotton towels, and the soap that the women had left for them.

"Go ahead," Gabe said, "use it."

"What are you going to do?"

"I'm going off to see if I can find them," Gabe said.

Alarm flashed in Meg's eyes. "Then I should go, too."

"No. I look plenty rough enough to be just another American outlaw on the run. But if you were with me in some of the places I'll go, it would only cause problems. And more important, everyone would remember you so that when the sheriff and that United States marshal come hunting for us, they'll have plenty of help."

From her expression, Gabe could tell that Meg did not like the idea of being left alone and yet, she was smart enough to realize that Gabe was right.

"When will you return?"

"By tonight. And if for some reason I don't, then I want you to ride on back to El Paso and hand yourself over to the sheriff or one of his deputies. Whoever is on duty when you get there."

"What?"

"If you do that," Gabe argued, "you might go to jail, but it won't be for long. If you don't do it, you'll spend the rest of your life looking over your shoulder. Maybe you could even strike a deal with the marshal. Tell him where the bank robbers were going in exchange for them dropping all charges against you."

"Would they do that?"

"I don't know," Gabe admitted, "but it would be worth a try."

Meg came over to stand beside him. "We don't even know each other's names."

"Gabe Conrad," he said, softly brushing her cheek with his finger. "I was raised by the Oglala Sioux. They call me Long Rider."

"Margaret Bryan," she told him. "But everyone calls me

Meg. I was raised in Houston, only child of a rich banker. I was spoiled rotten and was in trouble from the time I was thirteen but never trouble like I'm in now."

"You were kidnapped by those men," Gabe said. "They beat you half to death and raped you."

Meg hung her head.

Gabe started to turn and leave, but Meg threw her arms around his neck and kissed him on the lips. "Be careful," she pleaded.

"I will."

"And come back soon."

"Count on it," he promised, having to unlock her arms from around his neck so he could get out the door before his resistance crumbled to nothing and he forgot the reason he'd come to Juárez.

Gabe spent another of his precious silver dollars on a sombrero, sandals, and a serape. As he plodded up and down the dusty streets of Juárez looking for the three men who'd tried to kill him, he attracted almost no attention, except by the occasional person he stopped and tried to question.

Gabe quickly learned that the name Juara Escobar was extremely well-known and would always gain him an immediate reaction. Sometimes that reaction would be almost violent and once, a man began to curse and rant. He kept using the word *hermano* which Gabe suspected meant brother. It seemed a fair assumption that Juara had once killed the brother. The enraged Mexican might even have attacked Gabe if he had not somehow conveyed to the surviving brother that he was no *amigo*, or friend, of Juara Escobar but instead, an *enemigo* or enemy. Once that penetrated the Mexican's understanding, he fell calm and looked down at the well-oiled six-gun on Gabe's narrow hip.

"You kill heem, señor?"

"Si!"

"Bueno!"

The man got so excited that he grabbed Gabe's sleeve and began to yank on it and babble in Spanish so fast that Gabe did not even attempt a rough translation. But it was clear that the Mexican did know where Juara Escobar could be found, and that was all that Gabe needed to know.

The Mexican led Gabe south through the huge city, dodging between street vendors and, on a number of occasions, whipping and shoving whores away who tried to lure Gabe into sampling their charms.

It was evening when they finally came to a stop before a huge open plaza ringed by cantinas and little shops. In the plaza there were many people, and some of the young men were singing and playing guitars while señoritas in bright red and black dresses danced or swayed to their music. The Mexican's face darkened with fresh hatred, and he pointed to a group of men who were standing beside an outdoor cantina, drinking and laughing.

"Juara Escobar," the Mexican hissed, "asesino! Murderer!"

The man actually shoved Gabe forward, but he batted him away and held back.

"*Uno momento, señor, por favor!*"

The Mexican was not pleased. Perhaps he thought that Gabe was going to back down in fear. At any rate, he became so incensed that he tried to yank Gabe's pistol from his holster and shoot either Gabe or Juara, or perhaps even both. Gabe was much stronger than the outraged Mexican, and it was not difficult to shove him away, but when the man reached for his knife, Gabe figured the situation was out of hand. He stepped forward, and his fist crashed against the Mexican's jaw, knocking him backward over a small *carreta* loaded with a farmer's corn, chili peppers, and beans. The carreta tipped over, spilling its contents and the Mexican to the ground.

Juara Escobar and his friends were still some distance away, but they did look up to see what the excitement was. The guitars fell silent, and the dancing and singing stopped.

Gabe knelt and kept his head down so that his face could not be seen as he attempted to pick up the farmer's produce and appease the man for making such a mess. Unfortunately, both the farmer and the brother were incensed beyond reason and their loud cursing held the attention of everyone until Gabe had no choice but to stand up. The very last thing he had wanted to do was to brace Juara in a plaza filled with happy people and then try to either capture him or gun him down.

But now, as Juara looked closer at the tall man, recognition flickered in his eyes, and Gabe saw him stiffen with surprise and say something to his three friends, who placed their drinks on the bar top and flanked Juara.

Gabe shook his head because this sure wasn't the way he'd intended things to go. Now, instead of simply having to deal with Juara, he had three other gunslingers ready and willing to fight.

Gabe tossed the big sombrero and serape aside because he didn't want his gun hand to be slowed down even a fraction of a second. The thought of simply turning and fleeing into the dim alleyways and streets of Juárez to fight another day did not enter his thinking. He had come for Juara, Cass, and Ace, and the fact that Juara was the first he'd found meant he would be the first to either surrender or die.

The four Mexican banditos started walking across the plaza toward Gabe, and when the people saw their faces and the way their hands brushed the butts of their pistols, they scattered in fright.

Gabe stood his ground until he knew that there was no chance he could miss killing Juara and then, because the odds were so rigged against him, he did not wait for the Mexicans to choose their moment, but went for his own pistol first. He caught them by surprise. Maybe they thought he would beg for his life or lose his courage or in some other way disgrace himself. Maybe they were planning on making sport of the tall gringo before they shot his kneecaps apart. Gabe would never know because his left hand streaked across his flat belly and his cross draw was silky smooth and faster than the strike of a rattler. The six-gun bucked in his fist so rapidly that the six shots blended together in one long roll of gunfire. Juara Escobar was the first man to grunt and start backpedaling with a dazed look of disbelief on his swarthy, confident face. Two bullets stitched holes where his bandoliers crossed. Then Gabe tried to take out as many of the others as he could before they shot him.

Women shrieked, and Gabe heard the brother that had brought him to this plaza cry out in pain as a bullet found his body. Another bullet hit Gabe in the right arm and twisted him slightly so that he missed twice before his gun locked back on its targets and more of the banditos crashed over backward. The moment that Gabe's hammer fell on an empty cartridge, he threw himself aside, struck the earth, rolled behind the *carreta*, and reloaded, listening to the sound of running boots and people screaming.

Gabe slammed the last fresh cartridge into his six-gun and rolled again as one of the banditos suddenly appeared over him, firing wildly with his pistol. Dirt sprayed Gabe's face as he rolled again and pulled his trigger twice more. The bandito's face blossomed crimson and disappeared. Gabe came to his feet smelling gun smoke, and when the last bandito raised himself up from the ground and tried to fire, Gabe shot the man through the top of his head, then rolled back behind the *carreta.*

His heart was slamming inside his chest, but his mind was very ordered. There was no panic or fear. He listened and waited a moment, then stood with his gun up and ready to snap off another round as his eyes canvassed the now empty plaza. Nothing moved except Gabe, as he slowly crossed the plaza and came to a halt over Juara Escobar's body.

"I guess I'll just have to find Cass and Ace without your help, now won't I?"

Gabe reloaded his pistol and recrossed the plaza. Men and women moved cautiously out of hiding and stared at him in silence. The first ones to move were the little boys who raced over to the bodies of the four dead men and quickly rifled their pockets and took their guns, boots, and knives before they were chased away.

Gabe was pretty sure that, within an hour, the story of this gun battle would have spread all over Juárez and even into El Paso. Cass and Ace, if they were close, would hear of it and run, but the sheriff and the United States marshal would come for him loaded for bear.

He and Meg could not stay here another hour. It was not safe. They would have to strike out for California and hope that they would be there when Cass and Ace arrived, separately or together. In any event, going all the way to California was going to take some money and some time.

Gabe walked quickly as he retraced his steps to the little adobe hotel and cantina where Meg awaited him. He would have liked to spend at least one night in Meg's arms and enjoyed a little badly needed sleep, but those were luxuries he no longer could afford, so he did not torment his mind with them.

"Señor!" the hotel owner and bartender cried when he

pushed his way into the cantina. "You shot!"

Gabe had not even noticed his arm, so intent were his thoughts on how he and Meg had to get away in a hurry. But now that he looked at it, he saw that the arm really had taken a bullet, and he'd lost a fair amount of blood.

"*Por nada*," he said, "it's nothing. Just give me some water and . . ."

But the man was already racing back to his bar where he saturated his dirty bar rag with tequila and hurried back to press it against the wound.

Gabe clenched his teeth against the pain. "Hurts worse than the bullet did," he gasped, as he pulled away and went to the room to tell Meg that they had to leave on the run.

She was waiting for him in bed, and when he saw what he was going to have to pass up in the name of survival, he swore in frustration.

"Get dressed," he said. "I killed Juara. The word will be all over both Juárez and El Paso and bring the law running. We've got no time for sleep."

She jumped out of bed and hurried over to inspect his arm.

"It's just a flesh wound," she said, "but I should clean and bandage it before we go anywhere."

"No time for that," Gabe said, reaching for her clothes and handing them to her. "Get dressed now."

Meg did not argue, but did as he told her.

"Where are we going next?" she asked.

"To California. You can tell me where after we get across Arizona."

"Did you ask Juara . . ."

"I didn't have the chance to," Gabe said. "He died sudden. It was him or me, and there was no talk."

Meg nodded as she finished dressing and pulled on her shoes. "There will be other rooms and beds like this for us," she said. "Maybe even starting tonight."

"Uh-uh," Gabe said. "We're going to be covering a lot of ground in the next three or four days. What sleep we'll catch will have to be in the saddle."

Meg blinked, and when she saw the set, determined look on Gabe's face, she knew that he wasn't exaggerating one damn bit.

CHAPTER NINE

When the gunfight between Gabe and Juara erupted in the plaza, Cass went for his own gun as he dove for the floor. The señorita who had been on his lap spilled to the sawdust floor of the cantina and came up spitting and cursing, but Cass paid her no attention. He rushed to the open door of the cantina and flattened against it, very sure that he had been found and was under attack. The cantina adjoined the plaza, and when the gun smoke cleared, he saw Gabe standing with a gun in his fist, facing four dead Mexicans, one of them being Juara.

Cass wrestled with the decision to take a shot at Gabe. The distance certainly was within pistol range, but it would have been a chancy shot. He was just about to pull the trigger when it dawned on him that the best thing to do was to simply slip quietly back to his room, collect both his own and Juara's loot, and get the hell out of Juárez. Any man who was good enough to gun down Juara and three of his bandito friends was worth staying away from.

So instead of trying to kill Gabe from ambush, Cass decided that it would be better to run and hide. Maybe if he hadn't become a rich man thanks to their successful bank robbery, he would have made another decision. But money made a man a little more cautious, and Cass had too much to lose to gamble it all away now.

He retreated to the back door of the cantina, slipped into the alley, and was back at his hotel room in five minutes where two armed Mexicans stood guard outside his and Juara's door.

"What was the shooting about?" one of the guards asked him in Spanish.

"Juara Escobar is dead along with three of his friends," Cass said.

The two Mexicans, also banditos known for their ruthlessness and courage, were visibly shocked.

"But how can this be?"

"There is a man who is following us," Cass said. "A tall man with gray eyes and a twisted trigger finger. It was he who killed them and would kill me if he can. Would you like to make a great deal of money, señors? I know that you are both brave and very good pistoleros."

The two banditos nodded. "What is this man's name?"

"Gabe. That's all I know," Cass said.

"And how do we find him?"

"I think he will find us sooner or later. I am riding to California. I will pay you well to ride with me."

The two men asked for a moment to discuss the matter in private.

"I will go inside and gather my things," Cass said. "With or without you, I will leave now."

Cass unlocked the heavy door to their room, then closed it behind him and bolted it again. He quickly moved over to the steel chest resting beside the bed and from his vest pocket, he removed a key. When the chest was opened, he reached inside and hefted the bundles of cash.

"All mine now," Cass whispered, thinking how Gabe had actually saved him the worry of how to kill Juara and take all the cash for himself.

The sight of so much cash lifted his spirits and made Cass feel invincible. "Maybe he did me a big favor," he told himself out loud. "Maybe Juara would have tried to kill me before we left for California."

Cass smiled grimly. The two banditos just outside his room would even now be plotting how to kill him and take his money. Well, Cass thought, we will just see whose bones will whiten on the long trail to my new California rancho.

When Cass stepped outside with the saddlebags slung over his shoulder, his right hand was almost touching the butt of his gun. The two banditos, whose names were Pedro and Miguel, were smiling, as innocent as altar boys.

"We would like to know if we are now entitled to Juara's share of the money," Pedro asked.

"No," Cass said. "It is mine. You will both be paid very well—five silver dollars a day."

It was a lavish wage, more than most peons would earn in a month of back-breaking labor. Pedro and Miguel, however, were not impressed.

"But señor," Pedro complained softly, "we know that you have thousands of dollars. And without our help . . ." The man shrugged his shoulders and smiled sympathetically. His meaning was very clear.

"All right," Cass said, "how much do you want?"

"One thousand American dollars," Pedro, the heavyset one growled. "Half now, half when we reach the place you want to go."

Cass tensed, but only for an instant. What he could give, he could take back. And in truth, he did need these two men. They would know the secret places to hide, and if there was trouble either with Apache or other banditos, Cass knew they would probably be able to help him either fight or talk his way out of being killed.

"You win, señors," Cass said with a shrug of pretended resignation, "but we must go quickly. The sheriff and maybe even his deputies will hear of Juara's death and come here soon."

"Across the border?" Miguel's mouth twisted. "I do not think that would be so smart."

"Smart or not," Cass said, "they will come and we must be gone. So collect your horses and let's ride."

"First," Pedro said, "our five hundred dollars."

"Uh-uh," Cass replied, "not until we have escaped Juárez. "I will give it to you tonight, but not before."

The pair did not like this, but Cass knew that he had to make this condition or they might very well each collect five hundred dollars of his stolen money and simply disappear.

"You do not trust us?" Miguel asked in an injured tone of voice.

"No more than you trust me," Cass said.

The banditos laughed out loud and then relaxed and went to saddle their horses.

Fifteen minutes later, Cass vaulted into the saddle.

"Where are we going?" Miguel asked, jerking the reins hard to calm his dancing palomino.

"To California," Cass said. "Where the señoritas are hungry for real men and the skies are always clear and sunny."

Pedro laughed hard enough to display his brown, rotting teeth. "The women here are like that and so is the weather!"

"Lead the way!" Cass ordered. "Quickly!"

The two Mexicans were expert horsemen and well-mounted. Bristling with weapons, they galloped westward out of Juárez on an outlaw trail they had no doubt ridden hundreds of times on raids into Texas and New Mexico.

Cass felt good. He would use this pair just as long as they were of value to him. But one thing for certain, he would make sure that they never lived to see Modesto. It was funny how things always worked out different than a man figured they would. Exactly one month ago, he, Juara, and Ace had been broke and drifting toward Houston. They'd planned a bank robbery that had almost backfired and gotten them killed, and then they'd taken a pretty young woman for a hostage in some wild scheme to ransom her back to her father for a bunch of money. Hell, Cass thought, I must have been crazy to ever have even considered such a stupid plan. But no matter, the girl and Ace were gone—probably both dead by now—and Juara had been gunned down by a man who, by all rights, should have been dead.

It was strange, all right. Cass wondered about this gunman. How the man had ever survived the stomping in the head that Ace had given him was a wonder. But survive he had, and he'd come back to haunt them. Will he try to hunt me down all the way to California? Cass wondered. And what about Ace? Has he already killed that crazy, hotheaded fool?

Cass hoped he would never learn the answers to those questions. As far as he was concerned, with his saddlebags stuffed with cash and a ranch waiting to be claimed in California, he had everything going his way. He'd go straight in California. He'd become a gentleman rancher. Maybe marry a decent woman and raise a few squalling kids. He'd become a pillar of his community, maybe even the mayor.

Cass' thin lips curved into a tight grin. With money, a man could buy respectability as easily as he could buy whiskey or low-down women.

CHAPTER TEN

Gabe and Meg galloped due west for over a hundred miles across a harsh Mexican land. Fortunately, they saw no one until they decided to cross the border into Arizona and then they nearly intercepted a band of rustlers driving a large herd of stolen longhorn cattle. Gabe and Meg barely managed to dismount and pull their horses into the cover of some trees before they could be seen by the banditos.

"What will we do?" Meg asked.

"Wait until they pass," Gabe said, handing her his reins before he climbed up into the upper branches of a big cottonwood so that he could get a better view of the Mexicans and their herd.

From his vantage point high above the ground, Gabe could see for miles in all directions. He counted about twenty banditos driving at least two thousand head of cattle. Gabe had heard that cattle rustling was rampant along the border, but the size of this herd surprised him. He watched as the Mexicans whipped the sweaty longhorns through the scrub brush and down a rocky wash.

He was about to climb down when something else caught his eye and he stiffened, looking north.

"What is it?" Meg called up to him.

Gabe studied the cloud of dust to the north about a minute before he said, "Unless I miss my guess, it's the owner of the stolen cattle coming to reclaim his herd. Trouble is, he's only got three cowboys with him."

"Well that's his business," Meg said, "not ours."

Gabe frowned. Meg was right, of course. Whoever was coming after the cattle should have been able to read tracks well enough to know they were outgunned by the banditos at least five to one.

"Come on down," Meg said.

But Gabe shook his head. "I want to see what's going to happen. As fast as the cowboys are coming south, they ought to overtake the Mexicans before they can drive those longhorns more than a mile or two south of the border."

"But what happens shouldn't concern us," Meg said with exasperation.

"Maybe it shouldn't, but it does," Gabe told her.

Meg wasn't happy, but there was nothing she could do to make Gabe come down out of the tree. So she stood below holding their horses as the drama unfolded.

The banditos seemed to know they were being overtaken. A man that appeared to be the leader began making hand signals, and half of his men peeled off from the herd leaving just the other half to drive the cattle south. The leader and his men who stayed behind to fight yanked their rifles from their saddle boots and turned their horses loose. The horses fled after the herd, and the Mexicans took cover in the brush. It did not take a genius to see that the banditos were about to spring a deadly trap. With their rifles steady against their shoulders, they would easily annihilate the four cowboys that were rapidly closing on their backtrail.

"We can't just let this happen," Gabe said, dropping down from the tree. "It will be a slaughter."

To her credit, Meg did not object anymore. As she handed Gabe his reins, she said, "You're just a natural born do-gooder, aren't you, Long Rider? You couldn't stand to see me sent to prison, and now you can't abide watching an ambush even though it may mean that you're putting your own neck in a noose."

Gabe tightened his cinch. The ornery little Apache pony tried to bite him, but Gabe anticipated the move and batted the animal in the muzzle causing it to squeal in pain and anger.

"Stay here behind the trees," Gabe said, "at least until you got it figured out which way this thing plays out. If I go down, your best bet is to strike out northwest for Tucson."

"Without you, I wouldn't last a day alone in this wild country," she told him.

Gabe suspected that she was right. Still, he could not stand by and do nothing as the four Americans rode into a trap that they could not possibly survive. He mounted the Apache pony and drew his own rifle. He could not see either the banditos or the cowboys because they were blocked from his vision by a low hill. But Gabe knew that the trap was closing even as he whacked the barrel of his rifle across the rump of the pony and sent it racing ahead.

When he crested the hill, Gabe thought that he might already be too late because the four horsemen were charging headlong into the trap. Gabe threw himself from his pony. He was slightly off to the left of the nearest bandito and about seventy yards behind the main body of ambushers so they had not seen him yet.

Well, Gabe thought as he drew a bead on the nearest bandito, let's start hell's a'poppin'.

His first bullet caused a sombrero to go sailing off across the brush, and the man under it collapsed with a bullet through his brain. As the Apache pony raced off, Gabe levered another shell into the breech of his rifle and fired again. He missed the second time, but his bullet must have been damned close because now he had the banditos' full attention. They spun around and began to shoot at him. Bullets whistled all around him as he threw himself headlong into the brush. He rolled about six feet to his right and popped up again to see that the four Americans had also yanked their rifles free and thrown themselves from their mounts. The banditos suddenly found themselves in a cross fire with Gabe working his rifle to the left and behind them and the four unleashing a volley from directly in front. Another bandito caught a bullet and twisted to the earth in death. Now the odds were getting better. The banditos were confused. One tried to get up and run, but he paid for his cowardice with a bullet in the back that sent him sprawling into the brush.

A moment later, the fight was over. Gabe saw a white bandanna of surrender tied to the barrel of a rifle lift above the brush. In Spanish, one of the Americans demanded the banditos all stand up and raise their hands. The Mexicans had little choice but to do as they were told.

Gabe expelled a deep breath. Now it was time for him to look out for himself and Meg. But the problem was, his damned Apache pony had raced away and disappeared in the general direction of the herd of longhorn cattle. Gabe turned on his heels and started back toward Meg and the cottonwood trees. They could, of course, ride double for a short time. That was probably their only choice because he was not of a mind to go after the rustled herd of longhorns.

"What happened?" she asked as he came walking down the hillside.

"Lost my pony," Gabe said. "Let's get out of here."

"But . . ."

"There's no time for explanations right now; I'll tell you as we ride," Gabe said.

He grabbed the saddle horn and swung onto the back of Meg's horse. "Here," he said, reaching down, "give me your arm."

Meg did as she was told, and Gabe swung her up behind him as easily as if she were a child. He reined her horse around and sent the animal flying as a single rifle shot cut the air across his path. The horse planted its stiffened forelegs causing Gabe and Meg to nearly be catapulted over its head.

"Hold it right there!" a voice commanded. "Dismount!"

Gabe regained control of his horse. He knew it would be impossible to outrun the riflemen, and if he tried to fight, Meg might be shot by accident.

"What are we going to do?" Meg hissed. "He's wearing a badge."

"Yeah," Gabe said, "I just noticed. Guess we'd better do as he says."

They dismounted as the lone rifleman trotted toward them with his Winchester held out in front of him. When he came near, he said, "What's your hurry, mister? You saved our lives back there against those banditos. Figure we owe you our thanks." Gabe looked closely at the man. He was average-sized, tanned, and handsome with a long handlebar mustache and pale blue eyes under a ten-gallon hat. The badge he wore was that of a Texas Ranger.

"Well," Gabe said, trying to bluff it, "no thanks is necessary. But putting a bullet across our faces is a hell of a way to show your appreciation."

The man lowered his rifle but kept it pointed in Gabe's general direction. "Why'd you do it, mister? Why'd you risk everything to save us from riding into a trap?"

"Seemed like the only decent thing to do," Gabe said.

The Ranger turned his attention to Meg. "I guess you've got some explaining to do, miss."

"I don't believe I know what you're talking about," she said.

"Sure you do. We came to fetch you back to El Paso. Seems you escaped from jail. There's a United States marshal that's mighty interested in making your acquaintance."

Gabe expelled a deep breath. "If you take her back," he said, "she'll go to prison. That won't help recover the bank money."

The Texas Ranger shrugged his shoulders. "Then what will?"

"Letting us go on," Gabe said.

"Afraid I can't do that," the Ranger said. "There's almost forty thousand dollars missing between the two holdups. This young woman is the key to recovering that money. You can understand the problem."

"Sure I can, but taking her back is the surest way I know to lose that money. Judge Roy Bean says that—"

"Wait a minute! What has the judge got to do with any of this?"

"He sent me looking for the men that robbed the Houston bank."

"The Houston bank?" The Ranger shook his head. "You mean to say that bank robbery was committed by the same three men that robbed the El Paso banks?"

"That's right. Judge Roy Bean deputized me to bring them back alive—or dead."

The Texas Ranger was clearly amazed to hear this piece of news. "You got any proof of what you're saying?"

"I do," Gabe said. "The judge gave me this letter of authority as his deputy just in case I ran into this kind of trouble. He said that a sheriff might not accept it, but that any Texas Ranger would honor the commission."

The young man took the piece of paper from Gabe and read it slowly. Then he looked up and said, "Well, I'll be damned! This changes everything. Sure, we'll honor the judge's appointment of you as his deputy. And we'll even help you get your horse back."

"Be grateful if you'd just rope him and put my saddle on another animal," Gabe said. "That Apache pony is tough, but he is not to be trusted, and I'm tired of my long legs scraping the tops of the sagebrush."

The Ranger laughed. "All right," he said, "and we've still got a herd of cattle to overtake and bring back across the border. We could always use your help, friend. Especially seeing as how you're a lawman right now."

Gabe was not pleased to learn that he'd have to go help retrieve the herd, but all in all, he figured that he had gotten off pretty lucky. If this had been the United States marshal that the sheriff of El Paso had sent for, Gabe was reasonably sure he'd be wearing handcuffs by now.

CHAPTER ELEVEN

The other three Texas Rangers were a rough, hard-bitten bunch short on words and long on action. Their names were Slim, Bob, and Waco. Their leader was Captain Austin. By the time they rode back over the hill to rejoin the others, Slim, Bob, and Waco had disarmed the surviving Mexican banditos and ordered them to remove their boots and stockings.

"Turn 'em loose, boys," Austin ordered. "We'll pick what's left of them up on the way back with the herd they rustled."

When the banditos realized what was going on, they became very indignant, but when the Rangers drew their guns and made it clear that they would kill them if they didn't do as they were told, the banditos could not seem to get rid of their boots and stockings fast enough. The boots were collected and strung together across Bob's saddle horn.

Satisfied that the Mexicans were not going to walk very far in this rough country, Austin turned to Gabe, Meg, and his Rangers.

"I don't have to tell any of you that we don't have any authority in Mexico. What we do from now until we recross the border into the United States we do as private citizens."

Austin removed his Ranger badge, and his men did the same. "All right then, any questions?"

"Yeah," Slim said, thumbing his dirty Stetson back on his forehead, then using it to point toward Meg. "Why are we taking along a pretty young lady like her?"

"Because," the captain said, "we need this fellah, and he probably wouldn't ride with us unless we took her along. I just didn't think he'd appreciate leaving the lady here in the company of banditos."

Everyone glanced at the surly banditos and then back to Gabe, and they had to agree that the captain was right.

"Any other questions?"

"Yeah," Waco said, "how come he isn't under arrest? He and that girl are what we come looking for, ain't they?"

"We'd be dead or shot up by now if it wasn't for him," Captain Austin said. "That ought to be enough of a reason to overlook orders. Wouldn't you agree?"

Waco nodded his head. "It's just that we been together a long time, Cap'n. We all know how each other thinks and acts. Put a woman and stranger in amongst us, well, it just might mess things up royally."

Austin studied Gabe. "I guess what Waco is sayin' is that we need to know if you're willing to jump right in the middle of that bunch of cattle rustlers heading south. They won't surrender like this bunch. They got more to lose, and they'll fight to the man. There's still a lot more of them than us, and they're heading for the town of Pinos."

"How far south is it?"

"Only about twenty miles," Austin said. "It's a rustlers' settlement on the Rio Escondido. We'll try to overtake them but if we don't . . . well, it could get pretty rough."

Gabe twisted around in his saddle and looked at Meg. "What do you say?"

"Have we got any choice?"

"Nope," the captain said. "I need his help and you can give us all a reason to show off a little when we fight."

"And afterward," Meg said, her smile and fluttering eyelashes forgotten, "can we ride away free?"

Austin frowned. "I won't take you back to El Paso," he said, thinking it out as he spoke, "but I'm not sure that I can just turn you loose, either. There is still a little matter of forty thousand dollars of Texas bank money that has to be accounted for, and you seem to be the only one that has any hope of helping us retrieve it."

"Captain," Waco growled, "if we don't get after them, they're sure to make it to Pinos, and it'll be a lot rougher for us."

Austin tore his eyes away from Meg. "All right," he said, suddenly all business, "let's catch up the loose horses and give our new deputy one of his own. The others we drive straight through Pinos, if necessary."

As they started to ride away, one of the banditos cried in broken English, *"Señor, por favor!"*

"If God is willing," the captain called back to him and his dejected friends, "we'll be back for you in less than twenty-four hours. Best thing you can do is just to sit and wait, eh, señor?"

The bandito made an obscene gesture that caused Austin and his men to laugh as they galloped south after the big herd of Texas longhorns.

Nearly three hours had passed since the fight near the border. The Texas Rangers had dropped their carefree banter and were moving south at a steady, ground-eating trot. The tracks of the herd were very fresh, and Gabe could see a rising cloud of dust up ahead.

"We ain't going to catch them in time, Cap'n," Slim said. "Reckon we're going to have to whip the whole damn town of Pinos in order to get them damn stolen cattle back again."

Austin frowned. "I didn't think they'd be able to stay ahead of us so long. Those longhorns must have some jackrabbit blood in their veins."

Everyone looked to the captain, knowing he was the one that would have to make the decision on whether or not they would go into the bandito stronghold or return to the United States because the odds were too long to buck. Austin glanced toward the west. "Sun will be setting in about an hour," he said. "I'm thinking we ought to circle around to the west and come at them from the sundown side. They'd be half blind, and it might be easier."

"Either that, or we could hit 'em after dark, sir," Bob offered.

"Nope," Austin said. "In the dark we'll get all scattered. We'd be half likely to shoot each other once we get into that village. We either hit 'em at sundown, or we go home empty-handed."

Gabe could see from the hard faces of the Rangers that the idea of going home without the stolen herd of cattle was not one bit to their liking.

"How big is the village?" he asked.

Austin shrugged. "Let's see. Last time we burned it down, there were fifteen or twenty buildings, most all just shacks made of brush and scrap wood. I'd guess there were about forty men."

Even Gabe, who had fought long odds all his life, was shocked. "That's a lot of guns. Ten to one odds aren't too good."

"Well, that's true," Austin said agreeably. "But you have to remember that we left ten of 'em back near the border, and they were probably the best fighters. And the ones that drove the herd down here are likely worn-out and thirsty as hell. They'll have an hour to drown their aches with tequila. And hopefully some of the rest will already be drunk."

"So that cuts the number of fighting men down considerably," Gabe said.

"It does for a fact," Austin replied. "And if we could stampede that herd through Pinos, I'd say we had a real good chance of levelin' the son of a bitch without getting ventilated in the process."

"Then let's do it," Gabe said.

They made a wide loop around town and were in luck to see that the herd was between them and Pinos. With the sun sinking in the west, they formed a skirmish line just behind a low hill where they could not be seen from the village.

"They won't see us until we fly over the top of that hill and run smack into that big herd," Austin said. "So keep your guns ready but silent until they open fire. With luck, we can be right on top of them before they realize what is happening."

"What about her?" Slim asked.

"Miss," the Ranger captain said, "I think it's time for you to dismount and wait here until the dust settles."

But Meg surprised them all. "Captain, my father taught me how to shoot straight. I'd far rather be with you than worried half sick out here in the brush."

Austin looked to Gabe. "She's your responsibility. What do you say?"

"Let her come," Gabe said, thinking about how, when a Oglala village was attacked, the squaws would fight just as hard as the warriors.

"Suits me," Austin said, drawing his six-gun and glancing over his shoulder at the huge orb of sun that had just touched the western horizon and was firing the land with crimson and gold.

"All right, let's ride!"

They swept over the low hill. Both Gabe and Captain Austin made certain that Meg was still riding hard between them. The longhorn herd, although exhausted by the hard run from north of the border, saw the riders and bolted straight for the village.

The four Mexicans who had been circling the herd of stolen cattle were the first men to see the danger coming. With the herd stampeding all around them, they drew their guns and opened fire, then reined their horses and spurred hard after the herd.

So far, Gabe and the Rangers had not fired a shot. The village of Pinos was still almost a mile ahead of them, but they could hardly see it because the dust was so thick from the racing herd of cattle.

Two minutes passed, and then Gabe saw a shack explode as if it had been dynamited. Boards went flying in all directions as the herd smashed through first one building and then another, wiping out every structure in its path. He heard gunfire and screams, and when he and the Texas Rangers reached the town, his gun started dealing death. Banditos were running everywhere, and although some men were calm and trying to return fire, just as many were scrambling about in panic. Gabe saw what was left of a man trampled in the dirt. Then he felt a bullet whip-crack alongside his ear as a Mexican jumped into his path and began to empty his six-gun. Both Gabe and Austin riddled him where he stood and swept past, shooting, reloading, and fighting for their lives.

The dust was so thick that it was like fog only its particles were burnished by the setting sun. Gabe took a bullet across his right forearm, and another struck his saddle horn and shattered it like lightning would the stump of a pine tree.

A horse screamed in death, and Gabe twisted around to see Bob hurled to the ground and trampled under the hooves of the milling cattle. A boy of only about seven came running forward. Gabe spurred hard, reached down, and grabbed his arm, then slung him up behind his saddle. He did not have to tell the boy to hang on tight.

Gabe and the Rangers kept firing their guns until there were no more targets and the sun went down. The cattle, staggering with fatigue, heads down and tongues lolling out of their mouths, went to the Rio Escondido where they drank and then stood unwilling to go another step farther.

"Vamos!" Gabe said gently to the boy who jumped down and disappeared into the darkness.

Gabe rode slowly back toward what was left of Pinos. There wasn't much. Just boards and trampled rubble. The dust continued to hang in the air long after the sun went down. When Gabe dismounted, he led his horse toward the bonfire that was being fed by Captain Austin and what was left of his men.

"Glad you made it," Austin said grimly. "That makes four of us, including the girl."

Gabe turned to see Meg standing beside her horse. She was leaning against her saddle, and he whispered, "Captain, is she all right?"

"Yeah," he replied, "just a little shaken, I think. Bob and Slim went down pretty hard. Slim was trying to save her after her horse stumbled and she was on the ground. He got her back up into his saddle, but . . . well, he just didn't have time to help himself."

"I understand," Gabe said, moving over to the young woman. "Meg," he said, touching her shoulder, "are you all right?"

She turned and looked up, then threw her arms around his neck and hugged him tightly.

"Slim died trying to save my life, and he didn't even know me!"

"He was a good and brave man," Gabe said. "They all are. Now come on over by the fire and let's get a look at you."

Meg allowed him to lead her over to the fire. Gabe saw that she was all right, though badly shaken and a little scraped up from the fall she'd taken.

"Your arm!" Meg cried. "You've been shot."

"It's just another scratch," Gabe said.

But Meg insisted on binding the wound while Austin and Waco prowled around in the dark to make sure that no one was going to come sneaking back to Pinos and take target practice on them at first light.

"Them that lived are gone," the captain reported when he returned. "And there isn't a shack left standing. In the morning, we'll have ourselves a better look. Dust and the herd will be settled. We'll be starting back north as soon as we can. It wouldn't do to be caught by the Federales. They'd probably send us in chains to Mexico City where we might be lined up against an adobe wall and executed."

Gabe understood. "Meg and I will help you drive the herd north but once it's across the border, we'll be wanting to head west."

"And if that doesn't suit my way of thinking?"

"Then one of us will die," Gabe said, "and that would be a pity."

Austin studied him a long time. "I don't guess either one of us wants to kill the other, friend. But I got a responsibility to recover that money. If it isn't recovered, a lot of good people are going to suffer."

"We'll bring it back," Gabe promised. "Whatever hasn't been spent, we'll return, minus our traveling expenses. That's my promise."

"Where is it?" the Texas Ranger asked, turning to look at Meg.

"I don't know," she said, "but I think that the men who robbed those banks are heading for California."

"Why?"

"They just are," Meg said.

"Mind telling me where in California? It's not as big as Texas, but it's supposed to be a pretty fair-sized state."

Meg shook her head. "If I told you that, you'd maybe start thinking that you needed to come along."

Austin smiled sadly. "I never been to California. Texas suits me fine. And if you two are killed, there'd be no trail to pick up after you're gone. The men that took that money would get away free. You wouldn't either of you like that to happen, would you?"

Gabe and Meg exchanged glances.

"I wouldn't like that at all," Gabe said.

"Me neither," Meg admitted, her eyes shifting from the faces of one man to the next. "All right then, they are heading for a town called Modesto. I don't even know where it is. Just somewhere in the middle of California. Cass inherited a cattle ranch and farm there. That's all that he talked about while I was his hostage."

"What about the other man? The one that pistol-whipped you behind the bank?"

Meg shook her head. "I can't say for sure that he is also going to Modesto. But he talked about going there the night before he robbed the bank. He was crazy and wanted to show Cass and Juara that he could get more money out of a bank than they did. I think he meant what he was saying, and that's where he'll be, too."

Austin nodded and toed the earth for a moment. "You believe her?"

"I do," Gabe said. "I think she's telling the truth."

"All right," the Ranger captain said finally, "I'll let you go to California by yourselves. But if you don't get the money and let me know by telegram within say, a month, then I'll be coming to find you, and there's no place on earth you can hide that I won't find you. Understood?"

They both nodded.

"Good," Austin said. "Now lets see if we can find us a few blankets and get a little sleep before sunrise. We'll have a long day on the trail tomorrow, and if the Federales overtake us, we're going to be in more trouble than we can shake a stick at."

CHAPTER TWELVE

None of them slept well that night, and early the next morning after the sun peeked over the eastern horizon, they were all shocked at the amount of destruction they saw around them. Pinos had been flattened by the stampeding herd. The buildings had not been structurally sound, and when the cattle had slammed into them, they'd fallen as if made of sticks and cardboard.

"They'll come back," Captain Austin predicted. "They'll sneak back before we have been gone one hour. They'll sift through this rubble, collect the old busted boards, and start to tie and nail everything back up again. Inside of two weeks, you won't know anything happened here at all."

Gabe did not doubt the man. He helped find a broken shovel and pick and dug graves for the remains of Slim and Bob. Captain Austin said a few words about what good men they were and pinned their Ranger badges on their chests before they filled the graves and went to get their horses.

"Let's get the hell out of here," Austin growled.

Gabe and Meg could not have agreed more and were plenty eager to leave. Pinos might be raised again from its devastation but, to Gabe, it did not seem worth the bother. True, the village had been nicely situated along the Rio Escondido which was a year-round stream, and there were plenty of pretty cottonwood trees to offer shade during the hot summers, but there wasn't much else to warrant a village here. The earth was clay and had many rocks, making it almost impossible for farming, and there did not seem to be much grass for grazing either.

"How would they have fed those stolen cattle?" Gabe asked the Ranger captain.

"They'd have slaughtered a couple dozen for themselves, jerked the beef, and used it for trade. The main herd, though, would have been driven farther south where there are some fertile valleys with grass."

Gabe nodded and mounted the best of the Mexican horses they'd captured. He had never again seen his little Apache pony, and that was fine with him because the mangy beast had possessed a mean streak as wide as his shoulders.

"Let's go!" Austin said, turning away from the graves and mounting his horse. He jerked it around and spurred off toward the herd.

Meg and Gabe followed him and did not look back. Gabe had counted the bodies of fifteen banditos. Many of them had been trampled to death rather than shot. Fortunately, no women or children had been found, though Gabe knew at least one that he had managed to save.

The Texas longhorns bawled in protest as they were pushed, whipped, and forced out of Rio Escondido and headed back up the same trail that they had been pushed down the previous afternoon. The cattle were very unhappy. Still weary and hungry, they moped along as docile as sheep. That would change after they were rested and fed, but for now, their behavior could not have been better suited to the shorthanded Americans.

Gabe was not a cowboy, though he had worked on ranches as a bronc buster. He had also helped out on a few roundups, so he had a fair idea of what was needed to keep the herd bunched and moving.

Meg had no idea at all. Because the country was so dry and dusty and because her horse was the slowest, she kept falling behind and nearly suffocating in a cloud of dust.

"Hey," Gabe said, coming back to rescue her, "you've got to keep that poor horse of yours moving along better than you have been or you're going to suffocate back here."

"I can't get him to walk any faster," Meg complained. "And when he trots, it kills me! The entire insides of my legs are chafed raw."

Gabe cocked his right leg around his saddle horn and unfastened a spur.

"Here," he said, returning his foot to the stirrup and extending the spur toward her. "Put this on and see if it helps."

"I can't do it and ride at the same time."

Gabe supposed she was right. "Then let's ride over there by the river in the shade of that tree."

"What about the herd?"

"We'll catch up with them," Gabe said.

They trotted over to the Rio Escondido which was very low at this time of year. Gabe dismounted and helped Meg down. He glanced north toward the cattle and knew that he and Meg would not be missed for at least twenty or thirty minutes and that the herd was too weary, footsore, and hungry to offer the two Texas Rangers any resistance.

"Sit down on the sand," Gabe said, tying their horses to a piece of brush before removing his other spur.

Meg did as she was told. She was wearing a riding habit, and when she tipped her knee up to try and attach the spur to her boot, Gabe saw that the inside of her shapely calf muscle was very red and irritated.

"It must hurt," he said.

"Yes," she admitted, pulling up the habit to show him more of her leg. "As you can see, I'm chafed all the way up."

Gabe swallowed drily as he firmly attached both spurs to her heels. He cupped a little of the water from the stream and patted it on the inside of her leg.

"That feel better?"

She leaned back and sighed. "It feels wonderful," she whispered. "Don't stop."

Gabe removed his bandanna as Meg pulled her skirt up high and spread her legs. He dipped his bandanna into the water, wrung it out a little, then began to wipe the cool water up and down the inside of Meg's poor legs.

"You should have told us it was this bad," Gabe said. "Maybe we could have found some liniment or salve."

"Where?" she asked, pushing herself up on her elbows to watch him. "Where in the world could you find those things out in country like this?"

He tore his eyes from her pretty legs and mumbled something about grease from a rabbit he could shoot, but she wasn't really listening as she squirmed and lifted her skirt up around her hips.

Gabe went cotton-mouthed as he dipped his bandanna back into the stream and began to wipe the insides of her red thighs.

"Oh," she moaned, "that feels so good!" She sat up and then came to her feet. Before he quite knew what was going on, she was wiggling out of her skirt and then the rest of her underclothes and flopping back down on the sand.

"A little higher, if you don't mind," she said with a devilish smile.

Gabe stroked her thighs with the cool water right up to her middle, and when he saw his hand was trembling, he groaned with desire.

"What's the matter?" she asked, innocent as a babe. "You getting tired of this?"

"Yeah," he said hoarsely. "I guess I am."

"Then why don't you think of something else to do?"

When they were finished, they both rolled into the stream and washed thoroughly.

"I suppose that we had better be getting dressed and catch up with Captain Austin, huh?" she asked.

"Yeah," Gabe said with a wolfish smile, "there are a lot more streams and rivers we can play in between here and California."

Gabe was about to say something more when his eyes caught a column of dust rising about eight or nine miles to the south toward Pinos.

"What is it?" she asked, seeing his expression suddenly change.

"It's trouble," Gabe said, grabbing his boots and yanking them on in a hurry. "It's either the Federales or a whole bunch of banditos coming to settle a score."

Meg did not have to be told to grab her things and get back into the saddle. And with Gabe's spurs still cinched down tight on her boots, she was ready to make her pokey horse run.

CHAPTER THIRTEEN

Gabe and Meg took off after the Texas Rangers at a dead run. The Mexican Federales must have seen them because they also pushed their horses to their limits.

"How far is the border?" Meg shouted.

"Damned if I know!" Gabe called back. "But even after we cross it, there's no guarantee that those Mexican soldiers won't come right on across the same way that we did."

It took Gabe and Meg nearly a half hour of hard running to overtake the rustled herd of longhorns. When Gabe waved his hand in a signal to indicate they were being pursued, Captain Austin did not need a lengthy explanation. The Texas Rangers drew their guns, dropped back behind the herd, and sent the weary longhorns into a stumbling charge north for the border.

But the longhorns were footsore, weakened from hunger, and despite their best efforts, were in no condition to outrun the Mexican pursuers. Each time Gabe looked back, the Federales were gaining at every stride. There looked to be about twenty of them, and they had their pistols drawn.

"We ain't going to make it!" Waco shouted. "Captain, what do you want to do?"

"I say we've made it already," the captain shouted.

"The hell we have!" Waco yelled. "The border is still a good five or six miles north of us."

"Can't prove it by me!" Austin shouted. "As far as the Texas Rangers are concerned, we're on American soil and those damned Mexicans are trespassing."

Gabe figured right away what was going on and even though he had to admire the Ranger captain's audacity, he doubted that the man's bluff would play.

"You go on!" Austin shouted. "Take the woman and keep these cattle moving!"

"No sir," Gabe shouted. "Meg, you keep pushing them north. Just keep yelling and don't let them stop!"

Gabe saw protest rise up in Meg's eyes, but he ignored her and reined his own horse to a standstill, then turned it around, drew his Winchester, and joined the two Texas Rangers.

"Has this got any chance of working, Captain," Gabe asked, "or is this going to be another Custer's last stand with us being the Seventh Cavalry?"

"I don't know," Austin admitted, levering a shell into his rifle and then wrapping his reins around his saddle horn. "It all depends on how damn macho the officer leading that charge wants to be."

"Sure wish we had a couple of double-barreled shotguns," Waco said. "Might make a difference."

Looking at the pair, sitting on their horses grimly determined to face no less than twenty armed Mexican soldiers, Gabe could not help but feel a mixture of amazement and pride. He'd always heard that the Texas Rangers had more guts than brains.

"You can ride on," Austin told him without taking his eyes off the approaching soldiers. "This doesn't have to be your fight."

It took Gabe about a second to formulate his reply.

"Guess I'll stick," he said, levering a shell into his own rifle as the two Rangers pinned their badges back on their chests. Neither of the Texas Rangers offered any thanks, and Gabe didn't expect any.

The officer in charge was a young and handsome lieutenant, and Waco cussed a little then said, "I was hopin' we'd have some fat old veteran in charge, sir. These young ones can be tough to deal with."

"I know," Austin said. "They can let their pride get in the way of their good sense. If the shooting starts, I'll drill the lieutenant, Waco, you take his sergeant, and friend, you get the rest."

Gabe could not help but chuckle. "You boys are mighty generous."

Fifty yards out, the lieutenant raised his gloved hand and brought his troops to a dusty halt. He then stood up in his stirrups and yelled, "Americans, you are under arrest. That herd is on Mexican soil and the property of the Government of Mexico!"

"At least he speaks good English," Austin said in an undertone, before he shouted, "This is Arizona Territory and we are American law officers. You are all under arrest for trespassing!"

Gabe's jaw dropped and so did Waco's who muttered, "Now that's rich, Cap'n."

Austin shrugged his shoulders. "I always believed that if a man was of a mind to bluff, he ought not to do it in a half-assed way."

The lieutenant was incredulous. He sputtered for a moment and then yelled, "I give you one minute to drop your weapons and raise your hands!"

"And I, Captain Austin of the Texas Rangers of these United States of America give you thirty seconds to do the same, or we will begin firing."

The lieutenant swore in fury. "Are you insane?" he stammered. "Can't you count! We will annihilate you, señors!"

"Maybe," Austin said calmly. "But you won't be around to see it because you're the first one that is going to die. *Comprende, señor?*"

It seemed pretty obvious that the Mexican sergeant, like his cavalrymen, did not understand English, but he could guess by the angry and disbelieving voice of his superior officer that ultimatums had been given and that things were not going well. Furthermore, when Waco dropped the barrel of his rifle on line with his corpulent chest, the sergeant became very upset and began to plead in Spanish with the lieutenant.

"What's he saying?" Gabe asked.

"He is telling his superior that he should not act rashly, and that maybe they are on American soil. The lieutenant is fit to be tied. He's a hotheaded young fool who may get us all killed."

They sat their horses and waited while the lieutenant and his sergeant and then all of the soldiers began to argue in loud, desperate voices.

"Some leader," Waco said with contempt.

"Silencio! Silencio!" the lieutenant began to yell, and when his words were drowned out by the voices of his men, he drew his six-gun and almost died when Austin threw the butt of his rifle to his shoulder and started to pull the trigger. The officer's face paled, and he threw his gun away into the brush, and then his hands shot up over his head.

"Don't shoot!" he cried. "Are you mad?"

"Damn right I'm mad," Austin shouted. "Now, you know that herd was stolen by banditos. They are American cattle. So you turn your boys around and ride back to Pinos before I send you off to meet the Virgin Mary!"

"But . . . but señor! You destroyed a Mexican village! I cannot let this pass without some justice. It would mean my career!"

"Your career or your life, the choice ought to be damned easy," Austin said. "Now *vamos*!"

The lieutenant began to curse in Spanish, but it didn't seem to bother the Texas Rangers in the least. Gabe didn't mind either since his Spanish vocabulary did not include a lot of swearing. He guessed that the lieutenant was simply trying to save some face and maybe even his career before he retreated with his tail stuck between his legs.

When the lieutenant calmed down enough to speak to them in English, he said in a voice quaking with anger, "You may go but never cross into Mexico again."

"That would suit me right down to the ground," Austin said, "but you'd just better take care of your end of the dirty business on this side of the border. If you don't, you can tell that rabble down in Pinos we'll be back in force. And the next time we hit that village of snakes, we won't leave so much as a tree standing."

The lieutenant began to shake with fury, and Gabe thought the fool was going to go for his gun, but the sergeant grabbed his arm and the Mexicans all whirled their horses around and raced away.

"Well done, Captain," Gabe said. "I don't play much poker, but I'd never want to sit in on a game with you."

Austin smiled. "We better get after that herd and that girl. Guess they might really be across the border by now."

An hour later, the three men overtook Meg and the longhorns which had slowed to a shambling trot.

"Well," Austin said, pulling his sweaty horse to a standstill, "I guess this is where our trail forks."

"I guess so," Gabe said, looking at Meg. "We got an agreement, and I mean to uphold our end of the deal."

"See that you do. I'm taking you on your words of honor that you'll do your damnedest to return whatever money is still recoverable."

"Some will be spent," Meg said. "Ace wasn't a man who could hang onto money."

"I do hope you'll take our bargain seriously. I'd hate to see anyone as pretty as you go to prison," Austin told her.

Gabe was anxious to be on the long trail west to California, but Austin raised his hand and said, "I'm going to be talking to Judge Roy Bean next week. Anything that you want me to pass along?"

"Nope," Gabe said. "You can tell him that I lost his horse, but I guess he can have this one if I still got him when we return. Tell him Juara is dead because he wouldn't stand for being arrested."

"Did you really gun him and three of his compadres down all at once?"

"Got lucky, I suppose."

"I doubt it," Captain Austin said. "When we faced those Mexicans just now, you could have run away, but you didn't. I got a hunch you're Texas Ranger material. Wouldn't you agree, Waco?"

"Sure would," the Ranger said. "Course, he'd have to get a little meaner, but after he lives on a Ranger's pay awhile, that'll make him plenty mean."

Austin chuckled. "Seriously," he said, extending his hand, "get that bank money and come on back. We'll take you into the Rangers on the spot. Even stake you to a good horse if the judge insists on taking yours back."

Gabe tipped his Stetson. "That's a hell of an offer," he said with a twinkle in his gray eyes before he turned his horse and joined Meg in riding off toward California.

CHAPTER FOURTEEN

When Ace hopped down from the stagecoach in Yuma, Arizona, the temperature was over a hundred degrees. He was covered with dust and stank from days of hard travel in hot country. But still, he was lucky to be alive.

His stagecoach had been ambushed by a half-dozen Apache warriors, and if he and another sharpshooter named Bill Taylor had not been passengers, the Indians would have successfully overtaken the stage and murdered everyone. As it was, the driver of the stage had died of gunshot wounds and the shotgun guard had taken a bullet in his forearm.

"Mister," the shotgun guard said as he leaned against the wheel of the bullet-riddled stagecoach, "you and Bill Taylor sure proved yourselves on this run. If you want my job, you can have it. I'm quittin'."

"Not me," Ace said, his hand firmly attached to the satchel that held all the money he had stolen from the El Paso Bank.

"Then what about you, Taylor?" the wounded shotgun guard asked. "Pays fifty dollars a month."

"I wouldn't do it for five hundred dollars a month," Taylor snapped, his eyes repeatedly glancing down at the satchel that Ace was holding. "If a man gets scalped and tortured by Apache, all the money in the world won't do him any good."

Ace started to leave the coach in search of a room. He had had his fill of riding in hot, dusty stagecoaches. He wasn't exactly sure how he'd get out of Yuma, but Ace knew that he needed some rest and recreation before he even tried.

"Hey," Taylor called, "can I buy you a drink? We been through hell this past week, reckon maybe we helped keep each other alive out there."

Ace wearily turned to regard Taylor who was his own age and size. Taylor had been trying to make friends all the way from Phoenix and lately, he'd shown more than a casual interest in Ace's satchel of stolen cash. He made Ace nervous because he was obviously a man ruthless and bold enough to take chances.

During the Apache attack, Taylor had proven his ability with a gun. Ace figured Taylor, though not a professional gunfighter, was a man that bore close watching. Taylor reminded him of a lean, hungry mountain cat prowling for its next meal. Taylor had a quick smile—too quick—and the coldest pair of eyes Ace had ever seen in a man's face. He looked tough as rawhide. Only a fool would fail to see that he was a very dangerous man.

"Well," Taylor said, "how about it?"

"No thanks," Ace told the man. "I mean to get some food and a hotel room."

"Why that suits me fine, too!" Taylor said with sudden enthusiasm. "Where do you want to eat?"

Ace hid his annoyance. He had a lot of cash in the satchel, and what he really wanted to do was deposit it in the bank until he decided how he was going to leave Yuma. But if he made a straight line for a bank, it would make Taylor suspicious, and that was dangerous.

"I don't care," Ace said, curbing his anger.

"Well, I know a good steak house," Taylor said. "It's got a saloon on one side and restaurant on the other. It's right beside the Colorado River, and that makes it a little cooler. Come on, we'll go over there and get some food and then find us some rooms at the Yuma Hotel. I know the proprietor."

Ace guessed that he had no choice but to accept Taylor's invitation. So leaving the stage behind, they sauntered up the hot, dusty street. Ace was carrying his satchel and Taylor had a pair of bulging saddlebags in his left hand. The heat was so punishing that nothing moved unless forced.

"You ever been here before?" Taylor asked.

"Nope."

"Where you from?"

"Texas."

"Big state," Taylor said, looking sideways at him. "You have Apache trouble there, too?"

"Some."

Ace passed the Bank of Arizona and had to curb his impulse to go inside and deposit his money. He hoped the restaurant and saloon that Taylor had in mind was one of the next establishments just up ahead.

"I keep coming back here," Taylor said with a smile. "This town started out as Fort Yuma, and then it became Arizona City. Now, it's called Yuma after the damned Yuma Indians. Gettin' to be pretty damn big now. Lots of opportunity for a man with a little capital to invest and for someone who knows the lay of things."

"Is that right?" Ace said without interest. "How much farther is it to where we're going to eat?"

"Just up ahead there on the river. See, it's right there. Got good steaks and sometimes a pretty Mexican girl to wait on the tables. I could sure use some female company after that long stage ride we took. What about you?"

"I told you I was hungry, and I want a bath," Ace said snappishly.

"Hey," Taylor said, "I understand. It's fine to be grumpy. We just been through hell. But after we eat and have a couple of drinks, I guarantee that things will look rosier. There's two whorehouses in Yuma, and . . ."

Ace came to a halt in the middle of the street and turned to face his talkative companion.

"Listen," he began, "I know we fought side by side and did ourselves pretty proud against the Apache, but I'm a loner. So if it's all the same to you, I'd just as—"

"Hey!" Taylor said, clamping his hand on Ace's shoulder. "Take it easy, man! I just figured you shot a couple more Indians than I did, and I owed you a steak and a whiskey! That's all! After that, you can go your way and I'll go mine. Okay?"

Ace relaxed and suddenly felt a little foolish. The strain of the stagecoach attack and of keeping the satchel of money clenched in his fist and under his guard twenty-four hours a day was taking its toll on his nerves. This Taylor fella was all right. It was possible that he might even be helpful.

"Sorry," Ace grunted. "I guess I am a little edgy."

"Anybody would be in this dust and heat," Taylor said sympathetically. "Me, I'm more used to this kind of weather than a man from Texas. Heat doesn't rile me up at all. And as for cleaning up, well, I'd recommend getting a bar of soap and hopping in that river. It'll sure cool you off in a hurry."

"I'd prefer a bath," Ace said cryptically.

When they entered the steak house, the interior was probably about ninety degrees, but it seemed cool in contrast to the outdoors. Ace sighed in relief to be out of the hot sun.

The place was big, and the bar was backed by a plate glass window that overlooked the river.

"What's your pleasure, Taylor?" the bartender asked without much enthusiasm. "Whiskey?"

"Yeah," Taylor said. "A double—and the same for my friend here. We just got off the westbound stage. Killed us about ten Apache that made the mistake of jumpin' me and Ace, here!"

Taylor looked around the room at the men who'd stopped talking and drinking. He raised his voice. "Yes sir! They killed old Hank Piles, the driver, and they wounded Harold Long, the shotgun. If me and my friend hadn't been on board, the stage would have been taken, by Gawd!"

Ace saw the men nod with respect. "Say Taylor," one of the customers said, "why don't you and your friend hire on with the Southern Pacific Railroad? They'll be needing some good Indian fighters."

"No thanks," Taylor said. "A smart man don't push his luck."

The men laughed, and Taylor raised his glass of whiskey and held it up to the room.

"Here's to the day when every last Apache is dead—hell, when every Indian anywhere is dead!"

The men raised their glasses and matched the toast. Ace poured his whiskey down, and it felt hot and raw in his throat. It seared the lining of his stomach and made him gag but felt wonderful.

The bartender refilled their glasses saying, "Drinks on the house, boys! Anytime we can get rid of a mess of damn Apache, I'll pour a free round."

The patrons rushed the bar, and the next thing that Ace knew, he was surrounded by admiring men who were drinking and patting him on the shoulder. As Taylor had promised, he felt his spirits rise dramatically. Taylor bought a round of drinks for the house, and it occurred to Ace that he ought to do the same.

"Drinks on me!" Ace said, pounding his fist on the bar. "Set 'em up, bartender!"

"See, old buddy?" Taylor said, grinning. "I told you this was the happiest place to be in Arizona. Nice, friendly people, good food."

Ace could feel his head starting to spin a little, and it was no wonder. He had not had a decent feed in several days.

"I could use something to eat right now," he said.

"Sure, sure. But we'll get around to that quick enough. Say, Ace, what would you think about us going into some kind of a partnership?"

"A what?"

"A partnership," Taylor repeated.

"Doing what?"

"I don't know," Taylor drawled, "but I know this town, and there are opportunities aplenty."

He glanced down at the satchel that was pressed tightly between Ace's boots. "Of course, it would take a little money to get us started in on something."

"Sorry," Ace said, rubbing the inside of his boot against the satchel of bank money, "but I can't help. So why don't we just try and figure a way to get me to California?"

Taylor looked pained. "Now why you want to go over there for? Hell, I know that, if you had a little money to invest, I could . . ."

Ace was starting to get angry. "Listen, Goddammit, I said I don't have any money to invest. Now how in the hell do I get to California if the stage won't go on because of the damned Indians?"

Taylor's cheeks reddened, but he said, "The steam packet might be the only way."

"What the hell is that?"

"It travels up and down this river between Ehrenberg about seventy miles north and the Gulf of California down south."

Ace wiped the sweat from his brow with the back of his hand.

"This packet," he said, "after it gets down to the Gulf of California, then what?"

"Why, it goes around the Baja Peninsula and out of the Gulf into the Pacific Ocean. After that, it churns its way north to San Diego, then to Los Angeles, and finally to San Francisco."

Ace was suddenly all ears. "This packet, how long does it take it to reach San Francisco from here?"

"About a week. But it costs hundred dollars and—"

Ace smiled. "Never mind that. When is it leavin' next?"

"Leaves twice a week," Taylor said, his smile dissolving. "I thought you said that you didn't have any money."

"Well, I got a little," Ace said, avoiding the man's eyes.

Taylor nodded and then ordered them another round of drinks. Ace soon lost track of time, but not the satchel of money that he kept on the floor pinned between his boots. When someone jostled him once and he did move, he quickly regained his original position at the bar and stood his ground.

During the course of the next hour, he must have glanced down at the satchel fifty times. But amazingly, with his head spinning and the noisy crowd pushing and shoving all around him, he finally looked down one time to see that the satchel was somehow different. So different in fact, that when he bent over to study it, he saw that it was the wrong color! His satchel had been brown; this one was black!

A cold pail of icy water tossed in his face could not have sobered him up quicker. With a roar, Ace shoved men aside, dropped to his hands and knees, tore open the black satchel and stared at a man's collection of dirty, stinking underwear crammed inside.

"Who took it?" Ace screamed, jumping to his feet and flinging the dirty underwear overhead.

The other patrons staggered back in confusion and batted the underwear from their heads and shoulders.

"What's wrong?" one of them finally asked.

Ace blinked, and his eyes were bloodshot and wild.

"What's wrong? My money is gone!" he screamed, yanking his six-gun from his holster and cocking back the hammer as men whirled and raced for the door or threw themselves behind overturned tables.

"Come back here!" Ace shouted. "Which one of you took it?"

No one answered him. Ace cursed until the veins stood out in his face. Then he turned and aimed his pistol at the bartender.

In a low, deadly voice, he grated, "Where is it?"

"I don't know what the hell you're talking about!"

"My satchel!" Ace hollered, the gun shaking in one fist and the empty black satchel in the other. "It was on the floor right between my feet, and now it's gone. It was brown, and it had all my money inside."

The bartender, a heavyset, sweaty man with a large mole between his eyes, shook his head.

"Mister, I work this side of the bar! I swear I don't know where your money went."

Ace twisted around. "Where's Taylor?"

"He left about five, maybe even ten minutes ago," the bartender said. "I thought he was just going out behind the fence to take a piss."

Ace followed the bartender's glance, then he charged across the room and threw open the door.

"He ain't here!"

The bartender mopped his brow with the bar rag. "Mister," he said, "I don't know where Bill Taylor is, and I don't care. He's always been a thief, a liar, and a dangerous son of a bitch. But when he has money to pay for the drinks, I pour."

"Where?" Ace shrieked, the gun shaking in his fist.

The bartender's chubby hand passed shakily before his eyes. "I'd say you find him, you find your money."

At just that moment, they all heard the blast of a paddle-wheel steamer out on the river as it came into view through the back bar window and churned its way out of view moving downriver.

"Where's that going?"

"All the way to San Francisco, California, but its first stop is San Diego."

Ace hurled the empty black satchel to the floor and cursed before he staggered into a run. Outside, the bright sun caught him full in the eyes and it, along with all the whiskey, made his head begin to spin. He tried to shade his eyes and push on toward the river, but he fell hard and could not get back onto his feet. He raised his head as the paddle-wheel steamer's whistle screeched again in farewell.

"Damn him!" Ace choked, dragging himself over to a horse-watering trough and dousing his face in the water. "I'll find and kill that thieving son of a bitch!"

The bartender appeared several minutes later with a man wearing a badge.

"That him?"

"Yeah," the bartender said in anger. "He threatened to kill me and my customers. He owes me twen . . . no, closer to thirty dollars for all the drinks he bought and now says he can't pay for."

Ace twisted his head around to see a big sheriff standing over him with his gun resting on his wide hips. Ace wanted to raise his own gun and shoot the man and then kill the bartender, too, but he was too drunk and his vision was blurred by sweat and dirty horse water.

"Mister," the sheriff said, "I'm going to take your gun and put you under arrest. Don't try anything or I'll have to pistol-whip you, and that wouldn't help either of us."

Ace choked in helpless anger. He allowed the sheriff to take his gun and then help him to his feet. He could not take his eyes off the departing paddle-wheeler and said in a broken voice, "When's the next one leaving?"

"Friday, three days from now," the sheriff grunted, pushing him toward his jail, "but unless you come up with some money to pay for those drinks, you sure as hell won't be on it."

Ace gritted his teeth and said nothing. He was drunk, broke, and killing mad, but he had just enough good sense left in his head not to resist arrest and get his head cracked open. It was going to hurt bad enough tomorrow from the hangover he'd have anyhow, and he knew he would have to do some hard thinking if he ever intended to overtake Bill Taylor and his money.

As the sheriff hauled him down to his office, men came out to watch, and then the shotgun guard pushed into view. His forearm was swathed in bandages, and he was upset.

"Sheriff, why you arresting this man? He helped save my life and bring in the stage today. Why, if it hadn't been for him and Bill Taylor, we'd have all got ourselves killed."

"That's neither here nor there," the sheriff growled. "This man is drunk and disorderly, and he owes Mr. Peters here about thir . . . about forty dollars in drinks." The sheriff glanced at the bartender and winked. "It was forty dollars, wasn't it?"

Peters did not have to be jabbed in the ribs to understand that the ante had been raised and would go into their pockets. "That's right. Forty dollars is owed!"

The shotgun guard swallowed and said, "Well, I reckon that my employer just might pay that much in appreciation for what he and Mr. Taylor did to save me and the coach."

The haze lifted a little from Ace's eyes, and he said, "Ask 'em, for God's sake! I need to catch that packet before it gets away."

"Not a chance in hell of that," the sheriff grunted, pushing Ace inside his office and slamming the door behind them. Before Ace could say another word, the sheriff had the jail cell door open and was pushing him inside. The cell door locked upon closing, and the sheriff tromped back to open the door.

"You see if you can get that forty dollars, you hear now?" the sheriff could be overheard to say. "I don't want to keep this man locked up any longer than I have to."

"I'll sure try and get it," the shotgun guard promised. "Why, I'll send a telegram off this very hour!"

"Do that, and, Harold, what about this bullshit I'm hearing that you won't go any farther west?"

"Ain't bullshit," Harold swore. "We just barely kept ourselves from getting scalped by the Apache, and now the damned Yuma Indians to the west of us are on the warpath, too!"

"Jeezus!" the sheriff swore. "You just find a way to tell your bosses that we need a damned stagecoach connection! Can't be dependent for everything on just two steamers a week!"

"Yes, sir!" Harold swore. "I'll do it."

Inside the cell, Ace cradled his head and rocked back and forth with frustration and anger. What a mess he had allowed himself to be sucked up into! He'd just bet that Taylor had seen through him all the way and set him up real good in that bar with all those drinks.

"I'll find him and kill him!" Ace swore through his clenched teeth. "I'll gut-shoot him, and he'll die slow!"

"Hey," the big sheriff growled, "enough of that talk. If Harold gets the forty dollars, you'll be out of here as soon as you're sober, and then I want you out of Yuma, hear me now?"

Ace didn't answer because he couldn't. When he opened his mouth, he was suddenly so ill that he vomited all over the cell floor.

"Jeezus!" the sheriff raged. "Why you have to go and do something like that for?"

"Because I'm sick, you big, dumb son of a bitch!"

"Don't you swear at me, you miserable, drunken bastard!" the sheriff hollered. "You just messed up my cell and stunk up my whole damn office. I ain't going to clean it up—you are! And I swear . . ."

Ace didn't hear the rest because he was doubled over by another attack and was vomiting again. He had never been so sick and humiliated in his life, and he owed it all to Bill Taylor. Bill Taylor, who was right this very minute no doubt standing on the deck of that paddle-wheel steamer with a satchel filled with thousands of dollars clenched in his fist. Ace groaned as much from the thought of how happy and pleased Taylor would be with himself as from his own nausea.

"Sheriff!" he cried, weakly. "I've got to catch that steamer."

But the sheriff had gone outside because of the stench, and Ace was left alone to wallow in his own misery.

CHAPTER FIFTEEN

"Thanks for bailing me out," Ace said as he hurried down the street toward the stage office with Harold, the shotgun guard, rushing along on his heels.

"Now how many days will it take for us to get that stagecoach to San Diego?"

"Four days," Harold said nervously. "But the boss's telegram said we should wait until this Yuma Indian thing blows over. That might be a week or a month. The important thing for us to remember is that when you die, you're dead a damn long time!"

"Sure you are," Ace said. "But when you're broke, you might as well be dead."

"Yeah," Harold said, "I know that Taylor took all your money, but that don't mean we ought to rush out of here and get ourselves ambushed and killed. Now I know that my boss wouldn't want that either and . . ."

"I been thinking since I went to jail yesterday," Ace said, trying to block out his hangover. "And what I decided is that we can get to San Diego if we either take some extra riflemen . . ."

"Hold it, hold it!" Harold protested. "You won't find any men willing to cross that desert until this Yuma thing dies down."

"Or," Ace added, "we take along a little surprise just in case the Indians do attack."

They were nearing the stage line office, and Harold grabbed his arm.

"What kind of a surprise?"

"Dynamite," Ace said tightly. "We take along a few sticks of dynamite and blow any Indians we come across straight to hell."

"You'd start a war out there if you did that!"

Ace stopped before the stage line office. He could see an old man inside that Harold told him was a passenger agent, janitor, and general liveryman, and also a hostler who was in charge of taking care of the animals.

"Listen," Ace said, "we're leaving within the hour, and we'll need dynamite. But I'll promise you this—I won't use it unless I have to. You've seen me with a rifle and a pistol—I'm good. But if we get jumped by a bunch of them, then I'll blow the lot of 'em sky-high."

When Harold nodded his head with resignation, Ace said, "Now, all I need from you is to hear you say you can drive that coach to San Diego. Can you do that?"

"I . . . I think so."

"Good! And can you get the dynamite?"

"Sure, we use it sometimes to clear a road that gets blocked. There's a few sticks in the supply shack out back."

"Perfect," Ace said. "Now I'm going to jump into that damned river and clean up, then I'll be standing by the ferry waiting for you to drive the stage on deck."

Harold toed the dirt. "I sure wish you'd wait a week or two. If we did that, I could show you some things around here. You ain't been to the whorehouses or nothing."

"That's because I'm broke, and I've been in jail almost since I arrived in this hellhole of a town. Now I want out of here within the next hour, so you get that hostler of yours to hitch up his best horses, and you find us a couple of sticks of dynamite. If we get through, you'll be a legend and a local hero."

"But if I don't get through," Harold said, "I'll just be a dead fool."

Ace slapped the younger man on the back. "Get goin'," he ordered. "We'll get through and probably won't see a single Indian."

An hour later, they drove the stagecoach onto the Yuma ferry and were pulled across the lazy current by a team of draft horses corralled on the California side of the river. There were no passengers on board the stagecoach and no bullion to transport, only several bags of mail and some supplies that needed to be freighted to San Diego in a hurry.

"Let's go," Ace said, as the stagecoach rolled off the ferry. "I want to be in San Diego to meet that steamer when it churns into the harbor."

"What you gonna do if Bill Taylor ain't even on it?"

"He's on it," Ace said, "and I'll leave it to your imagination to guess what I'll do to him."

"The sheriff said you got sick and swore to gut-shoot him."

Harold adjusted the lines in his fist and cracked them against the rumps of the team. The horses bolted forward and started out west across the desert.

"Is that right, Ace?"

"It sure as hell is."

Harold stared straight out into the hot Mojave Desert that ran for better than one hundred miles.

"Well," he said after a long time, "I guess that Taylor probably deserves to die for stealing all your money, but I'd as soon you didn't make him suffer first."

Ace looked sideways at the kid and smirked, "Harold, don't let this come as too big a surprise, but I don't much give a damn what you think or want. Taylor is going to die in unspeakable agony. All you have to do is get this coach to San Diego before he arrives. You understand that?"

"I sure do," Harold replied in a small voice.

Twenty-four hours later as the stagecoach topped a low rise between the Chocolate Mountains, they were spotted by the Yuma Indians who gave chase.

"How many?" Harold cried, trying to look back over his shoulder and, at the same time, force his weary team of horses up the last few yards of the grade.

"About twenty, I'd guess," Ace said, reaching for the sticks of dynamite he had resting in the black satchel at his side.

They finally crested the mountain pass, and when Harold raised his whip to lash the team into a hard run, Ace grabbed his forearm and said, "Let 'em blow. They're not going to outrun those Indian ponies anyway, so we might just as well make our stand here on the high ground."

Harold twisted around to gape at the onrushing band of Indians. He nodded his head after a moment and said, "You going to use the dynamite on 'em right away?"

"Why not?"

Harold wrapped his lines around the brake and shook his head.

"I figure this will either scare the shit out of 'em or make 'em madder than hell."

Ace handed him a stick of dynamite as the shrieks of the Indians grew louder.

"Harold?"

"Yeah?"

"If you throw your dynamite before I do, I'll pull my gun and shoot you myself. Is that understood?"

Harold looked into his eyes and nodded.

"Good," Ace said, jumping up on the stagecoach's roof and motioning Harold to do the same. "Now just close your eyes and don't open them until I shout."

Harold closed his eyes. Ace waited, his feet planted wide and the hot wind striking him in the back. He saw a puff of white smoke erupt from the muzzle of an Indian's gun and then several more puffs of smoke followed, but he knew that the Yuma were wasting powder and lead. The range was beyond that of their pistols, and even he could not have shot accurately from atop a running horse.

Ace dropped to one knee when he judged the distance between him and the Indians to be one hundred yards. He cupped his hand and lit a match, touching it to his own stick of dynamite then to the one clenched in Harold's fist. The fuses sputtered, and Ace stood up again.

"All right," he said, "open your eyes, get on your feet, and count to three."

When Harold opened his eyes and saw how close the Indians were, he paled a little but held his stick of dynamite until Ace said, "Three!"

They both threw at the same instant. Harold was so scared his stick reached out the farthest. Ace saw the Indians try to turn their horses aside, but they had no time. When the twin explosions rocked the earth, obliterating the onrushing Indians and their ponies, all Ace and Harold saw was a cloud of dust.

"Holy smokes!" Harold whispered as the wind whipped away the smoke to reveal the remains of the Indians and ponies scattered across the barren mountainside.

Ace stared at the devastation for several minutes before he snorted and said, "I guess the Yuma won't be giving folks any more trouble for a while."

He had to grab Harold's sleeve and pull him around and then shove him down into the seat and hand him the lines.

"Harold?"

"Yeah?" the man said in a dead voice.

"I think the horses have gotten their wind back," Ace said. "We can push on for San Diego now."

"Sure," Harold mumbled.

They drove the team into San Diego and straight down to the wharf. Harold and Ace had not spoken since they'd dynamited the Yuma Indians, and when Ace jumped down to stride toward the wharf, Harold turned the stagecoach around.

Ace said, "You'll like being a hero when you get back to Yuma."

"I ain't goin' back," Harold said in a quiet voice.

Ace turned and looked out toward the bay. "We beat them, didn't we? Made it in just under four days."

"Yeah, we beat them. Ruined a good team of horses, but we beat them."

"To hell with the horses," Ace snorted.

Harold looked down at the man and then, without a word, he turned the team around and drove it uphill toward the stage yard.

Ace didn't watch the kid leave because every bit of his attention was directed out toward the harbor. He saw an old fisherman repairing a net and walked over to the man.

"Say," he asked in a light, conversational tone of voice, "when does the packet from Yuma arrive?"

The old fisherman looked up at him, then up at the sun, and finally out toward the Pacific. His face was brown and weathered. His hands were huge and thick from work. He raised a finger and pointed it out toward the ocean.

Ace followed his direction and there, coming into harbor, was the Yuma packet. Ace smiled and walked back up the wharf until he found a good hiding place. His stomach was growling and he was tired from the ride, but he felt curiously invincible.

From his place of hiding he watched the packet, a smile of anticipation frozen on his thin, cracked lips. When it finally docked, Ace saw that Bill Taylor was the first man to leap from the deck and come striding up the wharf wearing a big smile and carrying Ace's brown satchel full of money in his right hand.

Ace let Taylor pass him, and then he followed the man up the street a little ways before he drew up close behind him.

"Hey, mister."

Taylor kept walking, his mind happily engaged on how he would spend his huge windfall.

"Hey, Mr. Taylor?"

Now Taylor's attention was engaged. He must have recognized Ace's voice because he clawed for the gun on his hip. But he was wearing a seaman's heavy wool jacket so his hand never reached the butt of his Colt.

"You lose," Ace said, his own Colt bucking in his fist. Taylor's body jacknifed as if his spine was splintered and, indeed, it might have been. He twisted around, saw Ace's gun explode once more, then staggered, his gun slipping from his hands as he tried to hold himself up against the wall of a brick building.

"I'll take that," Ace said, snatching the satchel from the man's dying grip.

Ace opened the satchel and stared at the pile of greenbacks.

"Guess you couldn't have spent much of it on the steamboat, now could you?" he asked lightly as Taylor's mouth made gagging sounds. "Well, I'm off to Modesto now. So long!"

As Ace pushed his way around the man, he shoved him hard, and Taylor toppled into an alley where he gasped and then died.

A few people saw the killing, but they also saw Ace's deadly expression. No one interfered as the slender young gunfighter disappeared into the crowd, heading for the comfort of a hot bath, a good meal, and the most expensive whore his money could buy.

CHAPTER SIXTEEN

When Gabe and Meg finally rode into Tucson, the first thing they did was visit the livery stables.

"If either Cass or Ace is still here," Gabe said, "they'll have to have boarded their horses, and we'll recognize them."

There were only three stables in town and on the second, they got lucky.

"The tall, skinny man you describe," a liveryman said, "now I kept his horse here for almost a week. He was traveling with two tough-looking Mexican pistoleros. I kept their horses as well."

"What kind of a horse was the American riding?" Gabe asked.

"It was a tall, good-lookin' sorrel gelding."

"Blaze face and three stockings?"

"Yep," the man said, "that's the horse."

"He belongs to me," Gabe said. "That man and two friends he was riding with stole him from me over near the Big Bend country of Texas, near Del Rio."

"Well," the liveryman said, "the sorrel and the Mexicans' horses were hard used. The sorrel especially. He was thin, and he'd thrown a shoe. I shod him but not before he'd contracted a bruise on his right front. I tried to do a little horse trading for the sorrel 'cause I could see he just needed some rest and good feed to make a top notch ridin' horse. But the tall man, he wasn't interested in trading."

"Then he's gone?"

"Yep. Rode out with the pistoleros the day before yesterday."

"Toward?"

"Said he was heading off to Yuma. I told him the Apache were raisin' hell between here and there, and that even the damn Yuma were givin' people fits west of Yuma across the Mojave Desert."

"But he didn't care?"

"Nope." The liveryman spat a stream of tobacco juice into the dirt. "That man looked me right in the eye and said he'd get through to Yuma all right. Then I told him about the steamer that took passengers from Yuma downriver to the Gulf of California and then all the way around Baja and up the California coast. He seemed pretty interested in that."

"So am I," Gabe said. "I didn't even know such a thing existed."

"Well, it does," the liveryman said. "Sometimes that steam packet is the only thing that can get supplies into Yuma when the Indians are on the warpath."

Gabe looked at Meg. "I think this is where we ought to part company. I'm going on to Yuma, and there's no telling what kind of Indian trouble I'll run into."

"Indians or not, I'm going with you," Meg said. "But it's almost supper time, and these horses need a good feed and rest even more than we do. Let's stay the night and leave early in the morning."

Gabe knew that she was right. It made no sense at all to leave Tucson on half-dead horses. If he and the woman were jumped by Apache, they'd need animals under them that had the strength to run.

"All right," he said, "we'll leave first thing tomorrow."

That night, they shared a room and meal at the Stagecoach Inn. They ordered a bath, too, and that night when they fell into bed, they did not make love but went right to sleep. But the next morning just before dawn when Gabe awakened Meg, she was more interested in staying in bed with him than riding back into the Arizona desert.

"Wait a minute," she said, grabbing and pulling him close beside her, "can't we stay here another full day? If not for ourselves, at least for the horses?"

"Nope," Gabe said, feeling her cool hands sliding up and down his chest and belly. "Cass has two day's head start on us now. Maybe if we can reach Yuma before that steamer leaves for California, we can get him."

Meg began kissing his chest. She smelled good and felt even better.

"I just thought that we ought to rest one more day. Maybe the Apache will go away."

Gabe had to chuckle at that.

"Listen," he said, rolling her over onto her back, "I think we both know what you really want."

They made love slowly, with the sun coming up out of the east hot and white. When they were finished, Gabe started to get dressed.

"Meg," he said, "I sure wish you'd wait here for me."

"Can't," she said. "We're almost broke. I'd have to go to work in this town, and there aren't many things I know how to do except please a man."

Gabe shook his head. "Well then, I guess that's why you do it so well. I'll go get the horses and tie them up outside, then meet you in the diner. We'll have a good meal and be on our way."

In a half hour, they were eating a huge breakfast of steak, eggs, and flapjacks. When they were finished and had paid their bill, they headed straight for their horses.

"Hold up there!" a voice said.

Gabe stiffened and turned to see a sheriff standing on the boardwalk.

"You the man called Conrad?" the sheriff asked.

Gabe looked to Meg, then back to the sheriff.

"Why are you interested?"

"It's my business to be interested in who passes through my town. I got word that a man and a woman fitting your description escaped from the jail in El Paso."

"How about that?"

Gabe looked up and down the street. It was still very early, and nobody was out watching them.

"Would you be that pair?" the sheriff asked.

"Nope."

The sheriff's hand reached for his gun, but Gabe's own left hand was already streaking across his waist, and he drew his Colt in a smooth cross draw that froze the lawman.

"Are you crazy?" the sheriff hissed. "You shoot me down, and you'll never even get a boot in your stirrup."

Gabe stepped forward, grabbed the man by the shirtfront, and pushed him off the boardwalk in between a pair of buildings.

"Meg, get me my rope!"

"What the hell are you going to do?" the lawman sputtered.

Meg threw Gabe his rope and said, "Nobody's coming yet."

"Good!" He tightened the noose on his rope and said, "Stick your hands out, wrists together."

"The hell with you!"

Gabe shrugged his broad shoulders. “I don’t know why lawmen are always so hardheaded.”

“Well . . .” The sheriff never finished his sentence because Gabe palmed his six-gun and batted the man across the side of the head, knocking him out cold.

“Let’s get out of here before he wakes up,” Gabe said, recoiling his rope and tying it to his saddle before he mounted.

“I’ll tell you one thing,” Meg said with a shake of her head, “if I ever return to my hometown in Houston, I’ll sure travel a different way back.”

“Might be a real good idea,” Gabe told her as they reined their horses west and rode out of Tucson.

Two days later, they saw buzzards circling in the cloudless sky about three miles straight ahead of them. Gabe immediately felt the hair on the back of his neck stand up.

“What do you think?” Meg asked, her voice tight with worry.

“I think we’d better keep our eyes and ears open,” Gabe said. “Could be the Apache overtook Cass on my sorrel gelding and finished him off.”

“If that’s the case, they’ll have found all that cash that he and Juara took from the Bank of Texas. That would be bad news for us, Long Rider.”

“We’ll just have to wait and see,” Gabe said, angling his sturdy Apache pony off the main road so that his approach to the kill site was less predictable.

An hour of hard riding through rough country brought them up to the crest of a low hill, less than a quarter mile from where the carrion would be.

“Here,” Gabe said, dismounting and handing his reins to Meg. He pulled his Winchester from the saddle boot and looked up at her. “I’ll sneak up to the crest of the hill and get a good peek over the top. If there are Indians down there, we can back off and ride a wide loop around them."

Meg took the reins and dismounted herself. She watched Gabe clamber up the rocky slope and saw him drop to his belly and then slither the last few yards to the crest of the hill where he removed his Stetson and peered over. She waited with growing anxiety for nearly five minutes until Gabe edged back down from the hill and hurried to her side.

"Well?"

"There are two Mexicans down there surrounded by Apache. They're trapped in some rocks. One isn't moving and is probably as dead as my sorrel horse."

"Your horse is dead?"

Gabe placed his Stetson back on his head and looked up at the pale blue sky.

"The horse is what has attracted those damn buzzards overhead. My guess is that my sorrel probably went lame again, and Cass, rather than be slowed down, figured a way to kill one of the Mexicans he was riding with. Probably tried to kill the other, too, but the man got up into the rocks."

"So Cass took his horse and rode on to Yuma leaving the man stranded beside a dead horse."

"Yeah," Gabe said. "Cass was smart enough to realize the dead horse would attract vultures, and Apache would also be interested in seeing what all the fuss was about. So leaving the Mexican was just as good as shooting him only there would be no risk."

"How many Apache?" Meg asked.

"Five."

"So what do we do now?"

"That's up to you, Meg. If we buy into this fight, we'd be trying to swallow more trouble than we might want to chew. The Mexican isn't going to be the kind of a man we could turn our backs on. He'll be a killer."

"But we can't just leave him, can we?"

"He would kill us in a minute if it served his purpose," Gabe said. "But it goes against my grain to leave him here to be captured and probably tortured. I guess . . ."

Gabe's sentence ended abruptly as a sound of rifle shots interspersed with the lighter banging of a pistol filled the air.

"Be right back," Gabe said, hurrying back up the rocky hillside. When he dropped back down on his belly, removed his hat, and peered over the crest of the hill, he saw four Apache standing over the two Mexicans while the fifth Apache rifled through their clothes and removed their bandoliers.

"Well," Gabe said to himself as he eased back down the hillside, "that solves that problem."

"What happened?"

"They killed the second Mexican," Gabe said, checking his cinch and swinging back into the saddle. "I guess it's time we put some country between us and them, wouldn't you say?"

Meg nodded. She had not seen the death struggle but could well imagine it. That alone made her shiver in the heat as she remounted her horse and followed Gabe as he made a wide loop around the dead horses, dead pistoleros, and the victorious Apache.

CHAPTER SEVENTEEN

When Cass arrived at Yuma, he was riding a horse that was more dead than alive.

"How much will you give me for this horse and saddle?" he asked the stable man as he dismounted.

"Horse is worth almost nothin'," the man said, shaking his head at the poor, half-starved animal, "but that Mexican saddle is worth five dollars."

Cass nodded wearily. "Give me ten dollars for the both. You grain this animal, he'll come back."

"Seven dollars," the liveryman said stubbornly. "I won't be able to get him in shape for at least four months considering how run-down he is now."

"Okay," Cass said, just wanting to be rid of the horse. With his saddlebags full of cash, he didn't care a hell of a lot about the price. "Now when is the next steamer leaving out of here?"

"You just missed it," the liveryman said. "It left about six hours ago. Next one won't leave for another four days."

Cass swore in frustration. "I heard the Yuma Indians are raisin' hell to the west of us. That true?"

"Sure is. Ain't no stage going out until things settle down again." The liveryman smiled. "I guess your choice is either to wait for the steamer to leave or else buy a fresh horse from me and take your chances."

Cass seriously considered the second option, but he'd already escaped death once at the hands of the Apache and wasn't inclined to press his luck with the Yuma Indians. Not with his saddlebags bulging with cash and a ranch waiting to be inherited in Modesto, California.

"Guess I'll wait for the steamer to leave," he grunted. "Where's the best place to get a room and a meal?"

"Yuma Hotel will give you both," the liveryman said, "but they're damned expensive. Rooms are two dollars a night, with a hot bath and clean sheets. Meals are too steep for most."

"Just give me my seven dollars and point her out to me," Cass said, "and while you're at it, point me out the nearest whorehouse."

The liveryman chuckled as he drew a wad of crumpled dollar bills from his pocket and counted out seven.

"I guess you'll spend all this money before tomorrow. All but the fat or ugly whores cost as much as a room at the Yuma Hotel."

Cass took the seven dollars and patted his saddlebags. He winked and said, "I got a few extra dollars to spend."

He walked away and headed down the street toward the only two-story building in town, the Yuma Hotel. The sun was hot and fading in the west. Cass wished like hell that he'd managed to arrive just six hours earlier. If he had, right this very minute he'd be floating down the Colorado River toward the Gulf of California. In a few days, there'd be a cool Pacific Ocean breeze in his face and he'd be on his way to Modesto—wherever the hell in California that was.

In Yuma, the summer days were so hot that nobody stood outside in the sun unless they had to. All the storefronts had covered porches, and men sat in wooden chairs back in the shadows. Cass watched them watch him and hoped he looked like just another poor drifter with his dust-caked skin and threadbare clothes.

In the Yuma Hotel, he got a room, a bath, and then he shaved and had a good meal before he walked over to the desk clerk and said, "I'd like a woman sent up to my room, pronto."

The desk clerk was a man in his late thirties with a pointed chin, deep-set eyes, and thin lips.

"You want a woman," he said, "go on down the street a block, turn left, and you'll find a few ready to take care of your needs."

"Uh-uh," Cass said. "I just took a bath and shaved. I got clean sheets on my bed, and I want a clean woman. You understand?"

The clerk looked bored. "Mister, that kind of woman is in short supply in Yuma. But for the right price . . ."

"How much?"

"Ten dollars."

Cass dug into his pocket and from a wad of greenbacks, peeled off twelve dollars.

"Have her sent up right away."

"Yes, sir!" the clerk said, no longer looking bored because two dollars was more than he was being paid for working a twelve-hour shift.

Cass went to his room, kicked off his boots, and unbuckled his gunbelt which he slung over the bedpost. He rolled a cigarette and stretched out on the bed to smoke it. Ten minutes later, there was a soft knock at his door. He rolled off the bed, grabbed his six-gun, and went to the door.

"Who's there?"

"Milly," the voice said. "I was told you wanted some company."

Cass unlocked the door and stepped back with the gun out of sight. When the door opened and he saw a woman of about twenty standing in his doorway, he grinned. She was pretty, if sort of plump.

"Come on in, Milly," he said, closing the door behind him.

She took a quick glance around the room and then turned to him with a smile. When he stepped toward her, she retreated and said, "Money paid in advance."

Cass growled, "I already paid for you."

"I didn't see any money."

Cass grabbed the young woman's wrist and twisted it hard enough to make her cry out in pain.

"Honey," he said between clenched teeth, "I don't know what you and that fella downstairs are trying to pull, but it won't work on me, understand?"

Tears of pain filled her eyes and she whispered, "Please, let go of my arm! I'll get the money from him, mister. Just don't hurt me!"

Cass shoved her onto the bed. He licked his lips and then began to undress.

"Honey," he said, "I think you had better get out of that dress real fast, or I'm going to rip it off your chubby little body."

The young whore nodded vigorously and undressed as fast as any woman Cass had ever seen. Sitting on the bed, she swallowed and said, "You're going to be nice to Milly, ain't ya?"

"You bet I am. And if you're real good to me, I'll keep you four days and pay you fifty dollars and feed you downstairs."

Her eyes widened, and she forced a high, strained laugh.

"Well, well, mister. Sounds like you got some real money to spend."

Cass chuckled and then he crawled onto the bed. Maybe it was just as well he was stuck in Yuma for four days anyway. One thing was for certain, by the time he left for California, he was going to make damned sure that Milly earned every cent of her fifty dollars.

"Then he's still at the Yuma Hotel?" Gabe said, feeling his pulse quicken with expectancy.

"As far as I know, he ain't set foot outside of it in three days," the liveryman said. "He's waiting for the steamer to leave for California."

"When is that happening?"

The liveryman pulled out his watch. "In about two hours is all. But then again, Milly might get him to stay till the next one leaves. She's pretty persuasive that way."

The liveryman turned and walked over to a saddle rack. "This here is his saddle. That bay in the corral is the horse he rode in on. Neither one is worth much, but he must have money because he's had Milly with him ever since he arrived, and she's too smart to sleep with a man on promises. She'd want her money every day or she'd leave."

"Who's Milly?" Meg asked.

"Youngest and prettiest whore in town," the liveryman said. "Most expensive, too."

Meg looked as if she wanted to ask another question, but Gabe took her arm and led her outside of the barn and into the shade.

"It doesn't make any sense to go to his hotel room and shoot it out," Gabe said. "Especially since he's got a woman with him."

"So what are you going to do?"

"We'll wait for him down at the river. When he comes out of the hotel and down to the dock, I'll try to arrest him."

Meg shook her head. "I know him, Long Rider. He'll kill you. They say he's terrible fast with a gun."

Gabe frowned. "I'm not the slowest man that ever pulled iron," he said, "but I expect there are a few faster. I thought it was Ace that was the real gunslinger."

"Ace must be faster, all right," Meg agreed, "because Juara and Cass were afraid to face him in a gunfight. But Cass is good, too. And if he kills you, I wouldn't know what to do next."

"Sure you would," Gabe said. "I'll tell you this, Meg. You're a damn sight tougher and more self-sufficient than you give yourself credit for being. You'll do fine if I get killed."

"I'd rather not find out if you're right or wrong," she said. "Why don't you just get the drop on him and get the bank money back?"

"Okay," Gabe said, "I will."

She smiled. "Good! And I'll even help you."

"No thanks," he said. "In fact, I want you out of sight when he comes down to board the packet. Is that understood?"

Seeing that Gabe's mind was made up, Meg nodded. They climbed back onto their weary horses and rode down to the steam packet where they dismounted and tied their horses beside the dock. Gabe went to see the captain.

"Can you tell me if a handsome young gent left here in the last few weeks? He was about my height and weight."

The captain pulled at his muttonchop whiskers. "I don't notice if a man is handsome or not. Did this one have a gun tied on his hip and a lot of money?"

"Yeah," Gabe said, "he'd have had both."

"Then he was probably the man I took to San Diego on the last run. His name was Bill Taylor. I heard a gunshot just a few minutes after he disembarked. It was up the street, and when I passed there later, I heard that Bill had been robbed and murdered."

Gabe could not hide his disappointment. If this Bill Taylor was Ace and he'd been robbed and murdered, the money was as good as lost.

"Funny thing though," the steamboat captain added, "this Taylor fella got drunk one night and told a crazy story about a man named Ace. Supposedly the guy was in jail, but he'd be coming after him and . . . well, it was a drunken, crazy story and none of us paid much attention to it—then."

Gabe looked at Meg, then back to the captain. "But you've wondered since if this Ace fella was the one that followed you to San Diego. Is that it?"

"Yeah. You see, there really was such a man that got a young stagecoach guard to take him to San Diego so he could find Bill." The captain shook his head. "I guess we'll never know the whole story."

Gabe said nothing, but when he looked at Meg, he knew she had figured the story out just like he'd done. This Bill Taylor had somehow gotten Ace's money and then fled to San Diego on this steam packet. Ace had been waiting for him and his money when they'd arrived and had killed him.

"Here comes Cass!" Meg whispered.

"Get out of sight," Gabe said, turning his back so that his own face would not be seen.

The captain looked from Gabe to Cass. "Say," he stammered, "you're not going to have a damned shoot-out on my vessel, are you?"

Gabe did not answer, but when he heard Cass's boots closing on him, he drew his gun and whirled around to face the thin, wolf-faced gunfighter.

"Cass, I guess you've got some unfinished business back in El Paso with the law," he said. "Raise your hands."

Cass dove headfirst into the river. Gabe fired once but missed, and then he went into the Colorado after the gunfighter. Cass was still holding his saddlebags stuffed with money, but they were soaking up water and dragging him down. Somehow, he still managed to get his feet on the bottom of the river and would have climbed out except that Gabe grabbed his ankle and pulled him back into the water.

Cass swung the heavy saddlebags at Gabe's head. He clawed for his own gun, but Gabe's was already in his fist. He aimed, pulled the trigger, and hoped that the wet gun would fire. It did. Gabe's bullet knocked Cass backward. The man tried to yank his gun from his holster, and Gabe shot him again. Cass fell back with a splash.

"The stolen money!" Meg cried, jumping out from her hiding place and throwing herself headlong into the river.

The saturated saddlebags were sinking fast and going off with the river's current, but Meg caught them before they disappeared and came up sputtering and thrashing.

"I got it!"

Gabe holstered his gun and looked up at the captain of the steam packet and the astonished passengers and crew.

"It's a long story," he said. "I guess we'll have enough time to tell it to you on the way to San Diego."

The captain shook his head. "Are you a lawman?"

"Yes, I'm a deputy for the Honorable Judge Roy Bean of Langtry, Texas."

"Well you, those saddlebags and that young woman better get on this vessel before the sheriff of Yuma arrives or you're going to be in shit deeper than this river."

Gabe nodded with understanding and then waded over to Meg.

"I think we'd better take the captain's advice," he said.

"But what about our horses and stuff?"

Gabe pulled her out of the water, rushed over to his horse, and untied his mother's buffalo vest. He also untied his own saddlebags containing his mother's Bible and took his Winchester. Meg had nothing of value except the wet clothes on her back.

"Let's go!" Gabe called as he leapt on deck and the lines were cast free.

The captain did not have to be told twice. Perhaps he'd had a few run-ins with the sheriff of Yuma himself. At any rate, they were quickly off and steaming down the Colorado River.

"I'll catch hell for this next time I come back here," the captain said darkly.

"Not likely," Gabe said. "My bet is that the sheriff will confiscate our two horses and saddles and sell them for a nice piece of change."

"Are those saddlebags really filled with cash?"

"Yes," Gabe admitted, "but the money belongs to the Bank of Texas."

"What about your passage money to California? I don't take people on charity, you know. Me and my crew, we work hard and expect to get paid."

"Fair enough," Gabe said. "I expect that the Bank of Texas can spare us a little extra expense money as part of a reward."

The captain broke into a smile. "I'm looking forward to hearing your story," he said, meaning it.

CHAPTER EIGHTEEN

After weeks of suffering the deserts of the great Southwest, both Gabe and Meg found the cool Pacific breezes to be a tonic. They explained to the captain everything that had happened to them since they'd first met, except for the details of Meg's rape and her involvement in robbing the El Paso Bank.

"So you think you will eventually find this man in Modesto?" the captain questioned.

"It's our only hope of finding him," Gabe confessed. "Although I suppose he might still be in San Diego."

"No," Meg said. "It would not be like Ace to stay there if he thought that he could do better in Modesto. Besides, he was so proud of the fact that he'd stolen more bank money than Cass and Juara."

"Captain, where is this Modesto?" Gabe asked.

The captain pulled at his muttonchop whiskers. "I think it's in the central valley of California. South of the gold fields."

"We'll find it," Gabe said confidently. "It just might take us a little longer."

"If he isn't in San Diego," the captain said, "you could try the port of Los Angeles. From there, we go on to Monterey for a quick stop and end up in San Francisco."

"How long will we be in San Diego?" Gabe asked, studying the low brown and arid hills of the long Baja Peninsula.

"Twenty-four hours."

It was not much time to search the city for Ace, but Gabe took comfort in knowing that the man was not the kind to blend into the woodwork. Ace liked attention, lots of it. He'd be spending money and flirting with the prettiest women whose intimate favors his new wealth could buy.

No, Gabe thought, if Ace is still in San Diego, twenty-four hours ought to be long enough to find him.

"Look!" the captain said. "California gray whales moving down the peninsula!"

Gabe had never seen a whale before and, apparently, neither had most of the other passengers because everyone rushed over to the port side of the steamer to watch a pod of the massive creatures overtake and cruise past the steamer as easily as if it were dragging anchor. The whales were immense, some much larger even than the packet. They were covered with barnacles and undulated through the water, blowing tall plumes of water out of their dorsal blowholes. When their immense tail fins struck the waves, Gabe heard a great splashing sound. The captain smiled as his passengers oohed and awed with astonished delight.

"There used to be a lot more of them in these waters," the captain said, "but we've hunted most out."

"Look!" Meg cried, "There are some babies! Captain, where are they going?"

"The gray whales swim down the Pacific coast from the northern waters in the spring and have their young ones in the warm waters of the Gulf of Mexico. Then they return to the north in the late summer and early fall and they stay the winter. It's just the opposite of the birds."

Gabe greatly admired the whales. He had heard of their

existence, of course, but never realized how big they really were. To see them pass the northbound steamer as if it were standing still in the water made him realize how perfect the Great Spirit made his creatures, no matter what their size.

"I hope they do not slaughter them all like the Plains buffalo," he said.

The captain looked at him a little strangely. "Why do you say that?"

"Because, like you and these beautiful creatures," Gabe replied, "I remember how many buffalo there were on the Northern Plains only a few years ago."

The San Diego harbor was immense. As soon as they docked, the captain escorted Gabe to the sheriff's department where he introduced him to a Lieutenant Evans.

"He's a deputy of Judge Roy Bean," the captain said. "And he's looking for a man named Ace."

The lieutenant turned to Gabe, though he found it difficult to keep his eyes off Meg. He was young and ruggedly handsome and wasn't wearing a wedding band.

"Ace what?"

"I don't know his last name. But he's about my age and size. Kind of a flashy sort. He'd have a lot of money, and he'd be spending it freely. Problem is, the money belongs to the El Paso Bank."

"So there's a warrant for his arrest from El Paso?"

"I guess so," Gabe said, uncomfortably aware that there was definitely a warrant for his own as well as Meg's arrest in that hot border town.

"Well," the lieutenant said, "the sheriff is on vacation, but he left me ten deputies, and I'll ask them all about this Ace fella. Any distinguishing marks on him? Anything that might stand out at all?"

Gabe and Meg shook their heads. "Where will you be

staying in case my men can tell me anything that would help?" the lieutenant asked.

Gabe shrugged his shoulders. "Captain?"

"They'll be staying at the Nautical Inn tonight," the captain said. "It's where I'm staying."

"And after tonight?"

"If I don't find him before tomorrow at noon, we'll be sailing to Los Angeles," Gabe said.

"You don't give us or yourself much time, do you?" the lieutenant said, "but we'll do the best we can."

Gabe thanked the lieutenant who then turned to Meg and said, "I hope you'll be staying in our lovely city a good deal longer than your friend."

"I'm afraid not."

The lieutenant did not hide his disappointment. "I could show you Old Town and many of the sights here. San Diego is rich in history and has the finest climate in the world. It's a wonderful place to live."

"I'm sure it is," Meg said, "but I'm afraid we must be leaving for a place called Modesto."

"Modesto!"

"Yes," Gabe said, "have you been there?"

"I've been through it," the lieutenant said, "on my way out of the Gold Country. I'm not far off the mark by saying Modesto is not much good for anything except growing crops and a heat rash."

Meg laughed outright, but Gabe did not find the comment amusing. "Is it closer to Los Angeles or San Francisco?"

"Los Angeles. I suppose it's about two hundred miles northeast of that city."

Gabe frowned. "Well, I just hope we don't have to go there."

The lieutenant took Meg's hand in his own. "So do I," he told her.

Meg blushed, and Gabe just turned on his heel and walked out the door, saying, "She's in your care, Lieutenant, I'm going to cover this town from one end to the other."

"Long Rider, wait!"

But Gabe didn't wait. He'd waited long enough to even the score with Ace, the man who had almost kicked his brains out way back near the Rio Grande. And for another thing, he had a feeling that the lieutenant would be more than happy to look after Meg. Who could tell? Maybe something good would happen between them. Meg needed a good man, and the lieutenant seemed to fit the bill.

Gabe's stride was long and purposeful as he headed down to the waterfront and began to visit the rough saloons. It took him most of the afternoon to learn that no one of Ace's description had been spending big money on drink and fast women.

"You might want to try La Jolla just up the coast," a saloon keeper said.

"Why?"

"Because that's where the money in this town goes when it wants to play a little. They've got plenty of high rollers and casinos operating up there. A man with money can buy anything he wants."

"How would I get there?"

"Take the trolley," the man said, "makes a twice-a-day round trip. You could catch it if you hurry right outside."

"And there's no where else you can think of that a man who likes to spend money would go?"

"Sure, he could spend it right here in my place," the bartender grinned, "and tip me like a prince. But I guess that's just wishful thinking. Anybody flashing money down here on the waterfront would likely wind up swimming face down in the bay. Know what I mean?"

Gabe looked around the interior of the saloon. There were sailors of every nationality. Some of them were as rough and dirty as stray dogs. Even in his own soiled and tattered riding pants, shirt, and sweat-stained Stetson, he was comparatively well-dressed.

"Thanks for the free advice," Gabe said.

"Who said it was free?"

Gabe stiffened, but the bartender gave him a wide smile.

"I was only kiddin', mister. I can tell that you ain't loaded with money. Round-trip fare on the trolley is four bits. You got it?"

Gabe dug into his pockets. "I think so."

The bartender watched as he hauled out some change and counted it on the bar top.

"Yeah," Gabe said. "I got enough."

"Better get goin' then," the man said, "I can see the trolley coming down the street, and the old man who drives it don't wait for anybody."

"Much obliged," Gabe said as he hurried outside and jumped on the trolley. He paid the driver his money and took a seat. The horse-drawn trolley was all open with about fifteen wooden seats. The driver kept clanging a bell at every block so that by the time Gabe finally reached La Jolla, his head was ringing.

"When does the next trolley return to San Diego?" he asked before he disembarked.

"Eight o'clock tonight," the old man yelled.

"Thanks."

"Eh?" The driver cupped his hand to his ear, and Gabe realized the old man was half deaf from that damn trolley bell.

"Never mind!" Gabe shouted as he jumped down and headed along the top of a high sea cliff overlooking the most beautiful little cove imaginable. He strolled along the cove for a half mile totally lost in the beautiful scenery below. One sandy cove after another came into view, and each was more picturesque than the last. Seagulls squalled and soared on the ocean currents, and Gabe saw sea lions and seals dozing out on the foamy rocks just beyond the breakwater.

When he came to a huge old hotel, he turned right and walked up from a large cove and into what he could only have described as a bazaar with many different shops selling expensive goods from all over the world.

Gabe suddenly felt self-conscious at his shabby appearance because everyone he saw was expensively dressed. He saw handsome men with beautiful young women on their arms. He heard laughter, the soft bartering between wealthy merchants selling jade, ivory, oriental rugs, incense, rich tobaccos and perfumes. They spoke in many languages.

He was about to single out someone to ask about Ace when two large men dressed in white suits came forward. The largest one was gigantic and wore a full beard.

"Good afternoon," he said in a slightly Arabic tone of voice, "may I ask who invited you to this place?"

"Invited?"

"Yes," the man said, his smile dying, "this is all private property, and I must ask you to leave if you were not invited."

"He was not invited," the other big man said, locking his fingers on Gabe's arm. "Look at his clothes."

Gabe tore his arm away from the man. "It is true I was not invited. And if this is private property, then I'll leave, but not until I've satisfied myself that the man I am hunting is not here."

"You'll leave now," the giant said. He grabbed Gabe's arm and twisted it up behind his back while his partner grabbed and pinned Gabe's other arm.

Gabe was helpless to resist, but he struggled anyway and managed to kick over a tray of jewelry. The tray struck a white-haired woman a glancing blow and she screamed. The crowd turned to see what was the cause of the commotion and at that instant, Gabe saw Ace with a beautiful Oriental girl on his arm. Ace was dressed in a white suit and wore an expensive Panama hat which seemed curiously out of place because he was still wearing his gunbelt.

Their eyes met, but Ace did not react. Then Gabe was torn away by the two bouncers who hauled him kicking and struggling out onto the lawn overlooking the cove.

"You are a very disagreeable man," the giant said through his teeth, "and you need a lesson in manners."

The giant stepped back and drove his fist into Gabe's kidneys. The pain was excruciating. It brought Gabe to his knees. Then the giant smashed him wickedly across the face with the back of his hand. The blow had been aimed for Gabe's nose and, had it connected solidly, would have smashed his nose to pulp. Fortunately, Gabe had managed to turn his head at the last instant and caught the impact on his cheekbone.

"Don't come back," the giant said when Gabe rolled over on the grass and tried to clear his vision.

Gabe lay still until the pair disappeared back into the bazaar. He knew that he could not whip them both, that he had to focus his anger on Ace. He had to get back into that bazaar and find Ace before the man vanished once again.

CHAPTER NINETEEN

Gabe found that his legs were rubbery when he began to circle the bazaar. Each step caused him a stab of pain in the kidneys where the giant had punched him, and he took deep breaths to clear his ringing head. But in less than ten minutes, he located another entrance to the bazaar and was about to make a charge for it when he noticed the broad back of the giant standing guard.

A thin smile twisted Gabe's lips, and he moved quietly forward until he was within arm's reach of the giant.

"Excuse me," he said in a cheerful tone of voice.

The giant turned around slowly, and Gabe drove a tremendous uppercut into his solar plexus, just below the union of his rib cage. The giant's brown eyes bugged and his hands clamped on his stomach as Gabe let loose with a second uppercut. His knuckles ripped into the soft spot just under the man's chin, and the giant staggered back and then dropped unconscious into a huge potted plant.

Gabe rubbed his bruised knuckles and walked unmolested into the bazaar. If the giant's big partner wanted to fight, that was fine, but what Gabe really wanted was Ace.

"Excuse me," he said to a man wearing a flowing silk gown with embroidered tigers and dragons, "do you know where that man disappeared along with that pretty Oriental girl with the jade necklace?"

The turbaned head just stared through Gabe as if he was not present. Gabe frowned and went to a wizened little fellow selling oriental rugs. He asked the rug merchant the same question and this time, he received the response he wanted. The little man pointed upward. Gabe craned his head back and gazed up at the second-story balcony of the old hotel and saw Ace and the Oriental girl taking in the colorful view below with drinks in their hands.

Gabe had two choices—he could find the entrance to the hotel and then try to locate the correct room, or he could challenge Ace right here and now.

"Ace!"

Ace heard his name and looked down at Gabe who said, "Name's Long Rider. Remember? I'm the guy whose brains you tried to stomp into mush back in Texas. Thinking you had, you, Cass, and Juara took my sorrel gelding and left me for dead."

Ace blinked and recognition came to him with a jolt. But the man was cool and recovered quickly. Grinning, he said, "Well, well! Alive but brain-damaged enough to track me down. I wonder how—but I suppose it doesn't really matter."

"No," Gabe said, measuring the upward angle he'd have to shoot and wishing he had a better shot, "it doesn't."

Ace was standing behind a low, wooden railing and was visible from only the chest up. It was a tough shot. The good part was that Ace also had a tough shot. In order to bring his gun to bear on Gabe, he would have to lift it unnaturally high to clear the railing and then shoot downward. Gabe figured that, on balance, the railing gave him the advantage.

"Why don't I come down there, and we'll take a little walk to the cove?" Ace suggested. "No sense in anyone else getting shot."

Gabe smiled. "I generally hit what I aim for. Make your play."

Ace shrugged his shoulders. "I guess my lovely friend would be safer inside our room. Would you mind?"

Gabe shook his head, and the Oriental girl, with a terrified look on her pretty face, started to move past Ace. Something told Gabe that Ace would use her as a shield. He knew that the young gunfighter was ruthless and diabolical so Gabe went for his gun. The girl screamed as Ace attempted to grab her around the waist. She managed to throw herself out of the line of fire as Gabe's first bullet ripped up through the railing and drove wooden splinters into Ace's groin.

"Ahhhh!" Ace screamed as Gabe's second bullet cleared the rail and struck him like an uppercut. The bullet entered his handsome face just under the jaw and exited his skull up near the crown of his head.

Ace slammed against the hotel wall, then rocked forward and crashed through the balcony railing. His body did a complete somersault and landed on a glass display case of jade, ivory, and silver, sending exquisite pieces of jewelry flying everywhere.

Gabe didn't wait for the second bouncer to find him and attack. While women screamed and some of the bazaar's customers scrambled for the jewelry, he sprinted around a high brick fence and found the entrance to the hotel.

"Hey! What's going on out there?" a hotel clerk shouted.

"Somebody got shot!" Gabe yelled, taking the hotel staircase three steps at a time until he reached the second-story landing and dashed down a hallway.

He expected to have difficulty finding the correct room, but that problem solved itself when the Oriental beauty flew out of Ace's room with a bulging satchel in her hand. The instant she saw Gabe charging toward her, she skidded to a stop and reversed directions. If it had been a man, Gabe would have shot him in the leg. In this case, however, the legs were much too shapely to ruin so he tackled the girl in the hallway and tore the satchel from her grasp.

"Give it to me!" she shrieked, clawing for his eyes.

Gabe blocked her strike and swatted her with the heavy satchel. She cursed and then jumped to her feet and raced away like a frightened cat.

"Guess it's time to get back to Texas and Judge Roy Bean," Gabe said as he climbed to his feet and charged down the richly carpeted hallway after the Oriental prostitute whom he figured would know the quickest way out of this fine old hotel.

Five minutes later, Gabe was strolling along the seaside cliffs overlooking the Pacific. He guessed he might have to walk all the way back to San Diego and then there was the long, long road back to the Jersey Lilly, Judge Roy Bean, and Bruno, the bear. Oh yeah, and some tough Texas Rangers he'd given his word to about returning some bank money.

On a sudden urge, Gabe hiked down a steep trail to the bottom of a cove. He pulled off his boots and socks, his sweaty shirt, and finally his old Stetson and pitched them all into the sand.

Hell, he thought as he waded out into the cold, salty water, I never swam in an ocean before. May never have the chance to do it again, either. That Texas crowd could wait a few extra hours for him to enjoy himself.

Long Rider dove into the pounding surf, and when he came up, he let out a bellow of pure pleasure so loud it startled about a hundred seagulls and sent them protesting upward into the blue sky.

"Damn," he swore, using the salty ocean water to scrub the dust of a thousand miles of hard desert away, "this feels so good I think I might just spend the whole rest of the day here and not even start back for Texas until tomorrow."

BOOK ONE

(1864–1867)

It is my unhappy lot to write the closing entry in this journal.

Clay Halser is dead, killed this morning in my presence.

I have known him since we met during the latter days of The War Between The States. I have run across him, on occasion, through ensuing years and am, in fact, partially responsible (albeit involuntarily) for a portion of the legend which has magnified around him.

It is for these reasons (and another more important) that I make this final entry.

I am in Silver Gulch acquiring research matter toward the preparation of a volume on the history of this territory (Colorado), which has recently become the thirty-eighth state of our Union.

I was having breakfast in the dining room of the *Silver Lode Hotel* when a man entered and sat down at a table across the room, his back to the wall. Initially, I failed to recognize him though there was, in his comportment, something familiar.

Several minutes later (to my startlement), I realized that it was none other than Clay Halser. True, I had not laid eyes on him for many years. Nonetheless, I was completely taken back by the change in his appearance.

I was not, at that point, aware of his age, but took it to be somewhere in the middle thirties. Contrary to this, he presented the aspect of a man at least a decade older.

His face was haggard, his complexion (in my memory, quite ruddy) pale to the point of being ashen. His eyes, formerly suffused with animation, now looked burned out, dead. What many horrific sights those eyes had beheld I could not—and cannot—begin to estimate. Whatever those sights, however, no evidence of them had been reflected in his eyes before; it was as though he'd been emotionally immune.

He was no longer so. Rather, one could easily imagine that his eyes were gazing, in that very moment, at those bloody sights, dredging from the depths within his mind to which he'd relegated them, all their awful measure.

From the standpoint of physique, his deterioration was equally marked. I had always known him as a man of vigorous health, a condition necessary to sustain him in the execution of his harrowing duties. He was not a tall man; I would gauge his height at five feet ten inches maximum, perhaps an inch or so less, since his upright carriage and customary dress of black suit, hat, and boots might have afforded him the look of standing taller than he did. He had always been extremely well-presented though, with a broad chest, narrow waist, and pantherlike grace of movement; all in all, a picture of vitality.

Now, as he ate his meal across from me, I felt as though, by some bizarre transfigurement, I was gazing at an old man.

He had lost considerable weight and his dark suit (it, too, seemed worn and past its time) hung loosely on his frame. To my further disquiet, I noted a threading of gray through his dark blonde hair and saw a tremor in his hands completely foreign to the young man I had known.

I came close to summary departure. To my shame, I nearly chose to leave rather than accost him. Despite the congenial relationship I had enjoyed with him throughout the past decade, I found myself so totally dismayed by the alteration in his looks that I lacked the will to rise and cross the room to him, preferring to consider hasty exit. (I discovered, later, that the reason he had failed to notice me was that his vision, always so acute before, was now inordinately weak.)

At last, however, girding up my will, I stood and moved across the dining room, attempting to fix a smile of pleased surprise on my lips and hoping he would not be too aware of my distress.

"Well, good morning, Clay," I said, as evenly as possible.

I came close to baring my deception at the outset for, as he looked up sharply at me, his expression one of taut alarm, a perceptible "tic" under his right eye, I was hard put not to draw back apprehensively.

Abruptly, then, he smiled (though it was more a ghost of the smile I remembered). *"Frank,"* he said and jumped to his feet. No, that is not an accurate description of his movement. It may well have been his intent to jump up and welcome me with avid handshake. As it happened, his stand was labored, his hand grip lacking in strength. "How *are* you?" he inquired. "It is good to see you."

"I'm fine," I answered.

"Good." He nodded, gesturing toward the table. "Join me."

I hope my momentary hesitation passed his notice. "I'd be happy to," I told him.

"Good," he said again.

We each sat down, he with his back toward the wall again. As we did, I noted how his gaunt frame slumped into the chair, so different from the movement of his earlier days.

He asked me if I'd eaten breakfast.

"Yes." I pointed across the room. "I was finishing when you entered."

"I am glad you came over," he said.

There was a momentary silence. Uncomfortable, I tried to think of something to say.

He helped me out. (I wonder, now, if it was deliberate; if he had, already, taken note of my discomfort.) "Well, old fellow," he asked, "what brings you to this neck of the woods?"

I explained my presence in Silver Gulch and, as I did, being now so close to him, was able to distinguish, in detail, the astounding metamorphosis which time (and experience) had effected.

There seemed to be, indelibly impressed on his still handsome face, a look of unutterable sorrow. His former blitheness had completely vanished and it was oppressive to behold what had occurred to his expression, to see the palsied gestures of his hands as he spoke, perceive the constant shifting of his eyes as though he was anticipating that, at any second, some impending danger might be thrust upon him.

I tried to coerce myself not to observe these things, concentrating on the task of bringing him "up to date" on my activities since last we'd met; no match for his activities, God knows.

"What about you?" I finally asked; I had no more to say about myself. "What are you doing these days?"

"Oh, gambling," he said, his listless tone indicative of his regard for that pursuit.

"No marshaling anymore?" I asked.

He shook his head. "Strictly the circuit," he answered.

"Circuit?" I wasn't really curious but feared the onset of silence and spoke the first word that occurred to me.

"A league of boomtown havens for faro players," he replied. "South Texas up to South Dakota—Idaho to Arizona. There is money to be gotten everywhere. Not that I am good enough to make a raise. And not that it's important if I do, at any rate. I only gamble for something to do."

All the time he spoke, his eyes kept shifting, searching; was it *waiting?*

As silence threatened once again, I quickly spoke. "Well, you have traveled quite a long road since the War," I said. "A long, exciting road." I forced a smile. *"Adventurous,"* I added.

His answering smile was as sadly bitter and exhausted as any I have ever witnessed. "Yes, the writers of the stories have made it all sound very colorful," he said. He leaned back with a heavy sigh, regarding me. "I even thought it so myself at one time. Now I recognize it all for what it was." There was a tightening around his eyes. "Frank, it was drab, and dirty, and there was a lot of blood."

I had no idea how to respond to that and, in spite of my resolve, let silence fall between us once more.

Silence broke in a way that made my flesh go cold. A young man's voice behind me, from some distance in the room. "So that is him," the voice said loudly. "Well, he does not look like much to me."

I'd begun to turn when Clay reached out and gripped my arm.

"Don't bother looking," he instructed me. "It's best to ignore them. I have found the more attention paid, the more difficult they are to shake in the long run."

He smiled but there was little humor in it. "Don't be

concerned," he said. "It happens all the time. They spout a while, then go away, and brag that Halser took their guff and never did a thing. It makes them feel important. I don't mind. I've grown accustomed to it."

At which point, the boy—I could now tell, from the timbre of his voice, that he had not attained his majority—spoke again.

"He looks like nothing at all to me to be so all-fired famous a fighter with his guns," he said.

I confess the hostile quaver of his voice unsettled me. Seeing my reaction, Clay smiled and was about to speak when the boy—perhaps seeing the smile and angered by it—added, in a tone resounding enough to be heard in the lobby, "In fact, I believe he looks like a woman-hearted coward, that is what he looks like to me!"

"Don't worry now," Clay reassured me. "He'll blow himself out of steam presently and crawl away." I felt some sense of relief to see a glimmer of the old sauce in his eyes. "Probably to visit, with uncommon haste, the nearest outhouse."

Still, the boy kept on with stubborn malice. "My name is Billy Howard," he announced. "And I am going to make . . ."

He went abruptly mute as Clay unbuttoned his dark frock coat to reveal a butt-reversed Colt at his left side. It was little wonder. Even I, a friend of Clay's, felt a chill of premonition at the movement. What spasm of dread it must have caused in the boy's heart, I can scarcely imagine.

"Sometimes I have to go this far," Clay told me. "Usually I wait longer but, since you are with me . . ." He let the sentence go unfinished and lifted his cup again.

I wanted to believe the incident was closed but, as we spoke—me asking questions to distract my mind from its foreboding state—I seemed to feel the presence of the boy behind me like some constant wraith.

"How are all your friends?" I asked.

"Dead," Clay answered.

"*All* of them?"

He nodded. "Yes. Jim Clements. Ben Pickett. John Harris." I saw a movement in his throat. "Henry Blackstone. All of them."

I had some difficulty breathing. I kept expecting to hear the boy's voice again. "What about your wife?" I asked.

"I have not heard from her in some time," he replied. "We are estranged."

"How old is your daughter now?"

"Three in January," he answered, his look of sadness deepening. I regretted having asked and quickly said, "What about your family in Indiana?"

"I went back to visit them last year," he said. "It was a waste."

I did not want to know, but heard myself inquiring none-theless, "Why?"

"Oh . . . what I have become," he said. "What journalists have made me. Not you," he amended, believing, I suppose, that he'd insulted me. "My reputation, I mean. It stood like a wall between my family and me. I don't think they saw me. Not *me*. They saw what they believed I am."

The voice of Billy Howard made me start. "Well, why does he just *sit* there?" he said.

Clay ignored him. Or, perhaps, he did not even hear, so deep was he immersed in black thoughts.

"Hickok was right," he said, "I am not a man anymore. I'm a figment of imagination. Do you know, I looked at my reflection in the mirror this morning and did not even know who I was looking at me? Who is that staring at me? I wondered. Clay Halser of Pine Grove? Or the *Hero of The Plains?*" he finished with contempt.

"Well?" demanded Billy Howard. "Why *does* he?"

Clay was silent for a passage of seconds and I felt my muscles drawing in, anticipating God knew what.

"I had no answer for my mirror," he went on then. "I have no answers left for anyone. All I know is that I am tired. They have offered me the job of City Marshal here and, although I could use the money, I cannot find it in myself to accept."

Clay Halser stared into my eyes and told me quietly, "To answer your long-time question: yes, Frank, I have learned what fear is. Though not fear of . . ."

He broke off as the boy spoke again, his tone now venomous. "I think he is afraid of me," said Billy Howard.

Clay drew in a long, deep breath, then slowly shifted his gaze to look across my shoulder. I sat immobile, conscious of an air of tension in the entire room now, everyone waiting with held breath.

"That is what I think," the boy's voice said. "I think Almighty God Halser is afraid of me."

Clay said nothing, looking past me at the boy. I did not dare to turn. I sat there, petrified.

"I think the Almighty God Halser is a yellow skunk!" cried Billy Howard. "I think he is a murderer who shoots men in the back and will not . . . !"

The boy's voice stopped again as Clay stood so abruptly that I felt a painful jolting in my heart. "I'll be right back," he said.

He walked past me and, shuddering, I turned to watch. It had grown so deathly still in the room that, as I did, the legs of my chair squeaked and caused some nearby diners to start.

I saw, now, for the first time, Clay Halser's challenger and was aghast at the callow look of him. He could not have been more than sixteen years of age and might well have been younger, his face speckled with skin blemishes, his dark hair long and shaggy. He was poorly dressed and had an old six-shooter pushed beneath the waistband of his faded trousers.

I wondered vaguely whether I should move, for I was sitting in whatever line of fire the boy might direct. I wondered vaguely if the other diners were wondering the same thing. If they were, their limbs were as frozen as mine.

I heard every word exchanged by the two.

"Now don't you think that we have had enough of this?" Clay said to the boy. "These folks are having their breakfast and I think that we should let them eat their meal in peace."

"Step out into the street then," said the boy.

"Now why should I step out into the street?" Clay asked. I knew it was no question. He was doing what he could to calm the agitated boy—that agitation obvious as the boy replied, "To fight me with your gun."

"You don't want to fight me," Clay informed him. "You would just be killed and no one would be better for it."

"You mean *you* don't want to fight *me*," the youth retorted. Even from where I sat, I could see that his face was almost white; it was clear that he was terror-stricken.

Still, he would not allow himself to back off, though Clay was giving him full opportunity. "*You* don't want to fight *me*," he repeated.

"That is not the case at all," Clay replied. "It is just that I am tired of fighting."

"I *thought* so!" cried the boy with malignant glee.

"Look," Clay told him quietly, "if it will make you feel good, you are free to tell your friends, or anyone you choose, that I backed down from you. You have my permission to do that."

"I don't need your d——d permission," snarled the boy.

With a sudden move, he scraped his chair back, rising to feet. Unnervingly, he seemed to be gaining resolution rather than losing it—as though, in some way, he sensed the weakness in Clay, despite the fact that Clay was famous for his prowess with the handgun. "I am sick of listening to you," he declared. "Are you going to step outside with me and pull your gun like a man, or do I shoot you down like a dog?"

"*Go home*, boy," Clay responded—and I felt an icy grip of premonition strike me full force as his voice broke in the middle of a word.

"Pull, you yellow b——d," Billy Howard ordered him.

Several diners close to them lunged up from their tables, scattering for the lobby. Clay stood motionless.

"I said *pull*, you God d——d son of a b——h!" Billy Howard shouted.

"No," was all Clay Halser answered.

"Then *I* will!" cried the boy.

Before his gun was halfway from the waistband of his trousers, Clay's had cleared its holster. Then—with what capricious twist of fate!—his shot misfired and, before he could squeeze off another, the boy's gun had discharged and a bullet struck Clay full in the chest, sending him reeling back to hit a table, then sprawl sideways to the floor.

Through the pall of dark smoke, Billy Howard gaped down at his victim. "I did it," he muttered. "I *did* it." Though chance alone had done it.

Suddenly, his pistol clattered to the floor as his fingers lost their holding power and, with a cry of what he likely thought was victory, he bolted from the room. (Later, I heard, he was killed in a knife fight over a poker game somewhere near Bijou Basin.)

By then, I'd reached Clay, who had rolled onto his back, a dazed expression on his face, his right hand pressed against the blood-pumping wound in the center of his chest. I shouted for someone to get a doctor, and saw some man go dashing toward the lobby. Clay attempted to sit up, but did not have the strength, and slumped back.

Hastily, I knelt beside him and removed my coat to form a pillow underneath his head, then wedged my handkerchief between his fingers and the wound. As I did, he looked at me as though I were a stranger. Finally, he blinked and, to my startlement, began to chuckle. "The one time I di . . ." I could not make out the rest. "What, Clay?" I asked distractedly, wondering if I should try to stop the bleeding in some other way.

He chuckled again. "The one day I did not reload," he repeated with effort. "Ben would laugh at that."

He swallowed, then began to make a choking noise, a trickle of blood issuing from the left-hand corner of his mouth. "Hang on," I said, pressing my hand to his shoulder. "The doctor will be here directly."

He shook his head with several hitching movements. "No saw-bones can remove me from *this* tight," he said.

He stared up at the ceiling now, his breath a liquid sound that made me shiver. I did not know what to say, but could only keep directing worried (and increasingly angry) glances toward the lobby. "Where *is* he?" I muttered.

Clay made a ghastly, wheezing noise, then said, "My God." His fingers closed in, clutching at the already blood-soaked handkerchief. "I am going to die." Another strangling breath. "And I am only thirty-one years old."

Instant tears distorted my vision. *Thirty-one?*

Clay murmured something I could not hear. Automatically, I bent over and he repeated, in a labored whisper, "She was such a pretty girl."

"Who?" I asked; could not help but ask.

"Mary Jane," he answered. He could barely speak by

then. Straightening up, I saw the grayness of death seeping into his face and knew that there were only moments left to him.

He made a sound which might have been a chuckle had it not emerged in such a hideously bubbling manner. His eyes seemed lit now with some kind of strange amusement. "I could have married her," he managed to say. "I could still be there." He stared into his fading thoughts. "Then I would never have . . ."

At which his stare went lifeless and he expired.

I gazed at him until the doctor came. Then the two of us lifted his body—how *frail* it was—and placed it on a nearby table. The doctor closed Clay's eyes and I crossed Clay's arms on his chest after buttoning his coat across the ugly wound. Now he looked almost at peace, his expression that of a sleeping boy.

Soon people began to enter the dining room. In a short while, everyone in Silver Gulch, it seemed, had heard about Clay's death and come running to view the remains. They shuffled past his impromptu bier in a double line, gazed at him and, ofttimes, murmured some remark about his life and death.

As I stood beside the table, looking at the gray, still features, I wondered what Clay had been about to say before the rancorous voice of Billy Howard had interrupted. He'd said that he had learned what fear is, "though not fear of . . ." What words had he been about to say? Though not fear of other men? Of danger? Of death?

Later on, the undertaker came and took Clay's body after I had guaranteed his payment. That done, I was requested, by the manager of the hotel, to examine Clay's room and see to the disposal of his meager goods. This I did and will return his possessions to his family in Indiana.

With one exception.

In a lower bureau drawer, I found a stack of Record Books bound together with heavy twine. They turned out to be a journal which Clay Halser kept from the latter part of the War to this very morning.

It is my conviction that these books deserve to be published. Not in their entirety, of course; if that were done, I estimate the book would run in excess of a thousand pages. Moreover, there are many entries which, while perhaps of interest to immediate family (who will, of course, receive the Record Books when I have finished partially transcribing them), contribute nothing to the main thrust of his account, which is the unfoldment of his life as a nationally recognized lawman and gunfighter.

Accordingly, I plan to eliminate those sections of the journal which chronicle that variety of events which any man might experience during twelve years' time. After all, as hair-raising as Clay's life was, he could not possibly exist on the razor edge of peril every day of his life. As proof of this, I will incorporate a random sampling of those entries which may be considered, from a "thrilling" standpoint, more mundane.

In this way—concentrating on the sequences of "action"—it is hoped that the general reader, who might otherwise ignore the narrative because of its unwieldy length, will more willingly expose his interest to the life of one whom another journalist has referred to as "The Prince of Pistoleers."

Toward this end, I will, additionally, attempt to make corrections in the spelling, grammar and, especially, punctuation of the journal, leaving, as an indication of this necessity, the opening entry. It goes without saying that subsequent entries need less attention to this aspect since Clay Halser learned, by various means, to read and write with more skill in his later years.

I hope the reader will concur that, while there might well

be a certain charm in viewing the entries precisely as Clay Halser wrote them, the difficulty in following his style through virtually an entire book would make the reading far too difficult. It is for this reason that I have tried to simplify his phraseology without—I trust—sacrificing the basic flavor of his language.

Keep in mind, then, that if the chronology of this account is, now and then, sporadic (with occasional truncated entries), it is because I have used, as its main basis, Clay Halser's life as a man of violence. I hope, by doing this, that I will not unbalance the impression of his personality. While trying not to intrude unduly on the texture of the journal, I may occasionally break into it if I believe my observations may enable the reader to better understand the protagonist of what is probably the bloodiest sequence of events to ever take place on the American frontier.

I plan to do all this, not for personal encomiums, but because I hope that I may be the agency by which the public-at-large may come to know Clay Halser's singular story, perhaps to thrill at his exploits, perhaps to moralize but, hopefully, to profit by the reading for, through the page-by-page transition of this man from high-hearted exuberance to hopeless resignation, we may, perhaps, achieve some insight into a sad, albeit fascinating and exciting, phenomenon of our times.

Frank Leslie
April 19, 1876